D1562820

A TENT
IN THIS
WORLD

Other Books by William Weaver

Verdi, a documentary study
The Golden Century of Italian Opera
Duse, a biography
A Legacy of Excellence: the Story of Villa I Tatti

A TENT
IN THIS
WORLD

with an afterword

BY

WILLIAM
FENSE
WEAVER

McPherson & Company

1999

PS
3573
.E1992
T46
1999

Published by McPherson & Company, Post Office Box 1126, Kingston, NY 12402. Designed by Bruce R. McPherson. The publication of this book is assisted by a grant from the literature program of the New York State Council on the Arts. Typeset in Bembo. Manufactured in the United States of America. First edition.
1 3 5 7 9 10 8 6 4 2   1999   2000   2001   2002

Library of Congress Cataloging-in-Publication Data

Weaver, William, 1923–
    A tent in this world / with an afterword by William Fense Weaver.
        p.   cm.
    ISBN 0-929701-58-5
    I. Title
PS3573.E1992T46   1999   99-13466
813'.54—DC21   CIP

Printed on pH neutral paper. ∞

.

a Raffaele La Capria
grandissimo amico

In most books, the I, or first person, is omitted; in this it will be retained. We commonly do not remember that it is, after all, always the first person that is speaking. I should not talk so much about myself if there were anybody else whom I knew as well. Unfortunately, I am confined to this theme by the narrowness of my experience. Moreover, I, on my side, require of every writer, first or last, a simple and sincere account of his own life, and not merely what he has heard of other men's lives; some such account as he would send to his kindred from a distant land; for if he has lived sincerely, it must have been in a distant land to me.

THOREAU, Walden, page 1

S*eptember, 1947— Thursday.*

My arrival in Naples this morning was chaos. Strange that I had never imagined it that way, even in those moments when I tried to think with the maximum objectivity of what my first experience of Italy would be like, after four years of absence. Now that I am actually here, have really set my foot on the quay and fought my way through the customs, it is hard for me to summon up again those imaginings of mine. I suppose I pictured myself always as master of the situation: giving the porters exactly the right tip, ingratiating myself with the officials who opened my trunk, greeting Luigi and his family, who would have come to meet me, stepping into the waiting cab, and then sweeping through the city, the new guest.

Instead, this morning, when I looked over the rail at the swarming docks, confused with shouts, I forgot what I had imagined in the face of the overwhelming reality I saw in front of me. I got up at four a.m. to see our entry into the harbor. It was still dark

9

when I went up on deck, and I stayed there while the sun rose slowly from behind Vesuvius, lighting up the familiar bay, the islands Ischia and Capri, facing each other, unidentical twins.

Finally, when we were there, almost to the quay, I went down to breakfast, then to my cabin to tip the steward and arrange to have my luggage taken up. So far, everything was all right. But when I came out of the cabin, I found complete disorder. The lounges filled with people, most of whom looked suddenly unfamiliar. Bags arranged in piles: typewriters, cameras, even golf clubs. It looked like a dormitory at prep school on the day of graduation. And there was the same feeling in the air; passengers exchanged addresses, liberally invited to visit them other people who had been utter strangers ten days earlier; everyone was saying: "In case I don't see you again in the confusion of getting off, good-bye…" and they would shake hands, not knowing whether or not to feel sad, since they would no doubt see each other again in five minutes' time.

And, of course, the situation I had intended to master mastered me. At a certain moment porters swarmed aboard like raiding pirates, snatching up luggage and leaving the owners to struggle along behind as best they could, fighting their way through

10

the crowds, down the gangway to the dusty, teeming dock. Then, after the fight was over and one was finally on land, there was the terrible anti-climax, the interminable wait for the trunks to be unloaded from the hold. It was then that I realized, a few minutes too late, that an important event had passed me by: I had Set Foot in Europe again. The moment when I should have felt something significant, have made some gesture (Richard II kissing the English earth)—that moment had slipped past while I was making desperate arrangements with the porter to hunt up my trunk.

Beyond a wooden barrier was the crowd of people meeting the boat. Occasional shouts from those nearest the rail summoned the friends or relatives who came down the gangway. *Maaaaaaario,* and then an answering scream. And sometimes aborted conversation: How are the children? Is Mamma here? Was the trip nice?

I wondered where in that crowd Luigi was, or if he was there at all. He had written that he would meet me and I had sent him the date of my arrival and the name of the ship; but as I sat there on my suitcase, the confused mass of porters and passengers milling around me, nothing I had planned seemed real any more. The only reality was the monumental disorder

11

that surrounded me, the shouts and shoves and the language that I only partly understood. I was, suddenly, in Europe and I was a foreigner, more than I had ever been before. All at once I felt that I was completely on my own, with nothing familiar to rely on; and I was unreasonably, deeply afraid.

But soon my porter came back, hauling my trunk behind him on a little cart. And in a little while the customs men had gone through everything, putting aside the cigarettes and coffee, occasionally holding up something—a suit, a shirt—admiringly calling each other's attention to the fact that it was American. When I had paid the duty, the porter again heaved my trunk on to the cart and, with my suitcase and typewriter, pulled it through the gate.

Luigi shouted, recognizing me after four years, and I saw him elbowing his way through the crowd. And, in a minute it seemed, the trunk had been tied to the top of a taxi, the suitcase and typewriter put inside, the porter tipped, and we were sitting side by side, driving out of the port and through the city.

We hardly knew what to say to each other. "You've changed a great deal," he said at first. "You look so much healthier than you did during the war. You're fatter."

"You seem exactly the same." He does, too. It

was strange, seeing him now as he had been in those days in 1944, when I met him accidentally once while on leave and then got to know him well, visiting his family later during another leave, helping him with some translations from the English poets, meeting his friends. Strange that he hadn't changed at all, while I have changed so much. Not only that I have gained weight; I am a different person. In three and a half years how much has happened to me; I knew that he would ask me and I knew that I wouldn't be able to tell him.

From the window of the taxi I could see the city moving past. It, too, had changed. Places where I had remembered heaps of rubble were now bricked-up walls, there were no soldiers or heavy army trucks. In the Villa Nazionale women were wheeling baby carriages, a few old men were sitting desolately on benches; but the chicken-wire and the olive tents were gone forever, without a trace. Slogans were painted along the walls: Viva la Monarchia, Abbasso il Re, a hammer and sickle.

Luigi and I conversed about friends, what had happened to them, what they are doing now. Achille and Peppino are in Rome. Emilia is married and living in Milan. Carlo has a baby. The compact little group seems dispersed now.

Gennaro, the concierge, and his wife Rosina had been notified of my coming and greeted me enthusiastically. They, too, seemed unchanged. Rosina still thin and non-committal. Gennaro still fat and expansive, just a shade too expansive, with a kind of false friendliness that is almost servility. But he was always helpful to me in the old days, so it pleases me to believe that he is sincerely glad to see me again. He helped me get the trunk down to the apartment, where Signora Fabbri was waiting to welcome me.

She was also glad to see me, yet took my arrival as naturally as if I had just left the palazzo a few days before for a weekend trip to Capri. She is still the same: pleasant, stout, a little more chic than seems right for such a materfamilias type. She accompanied Luigi and me to our room, helped me put my things in order, fussing over me maternally, approving of the warm suits in my trunk because they will be good for the winter. After a while she went off to the kitchen to see about mid-day dinner.

Instead of unpacking I suggested to Luigi that we take a short walk before eating. First I wanted to look over the palazzo in which the Fabbri's have their apartment. It is late baroque, or rather *was*, because now it is something special and strange. Some political maneuver, the fall of some king, prevented the palace from ever being finished, so it was left half-done, some of the rooms without roofs, some with only three walls. Time and ivy and the sea, in which the front of the palace is set, have now had their effect and the building looks like a real ruin; but some of the apartments are beautiful, especially the Fabbri's with its large, high-ceilinged rooms and the terrace that looks across the bay to Vesuvius.

We walked around the corridors of the building, some of them paved with marble and some with earth, and then into the courtyard, where children were playing soccer. On the beach below the palace the fishermen were drawing in their nets, and their shouts drifted up to us, disembodied by the distance. Gennaro saluted us as we went out the gate and turned up the Via Posillipo, which follows the contour of the cape, set high above the level of the water and above the palaces and gardens which line the edge of the sea.

The weather this morning was wonderful: warm and mild. The air seemed thin, and I felt lighter and somehow immaterial; perhaps this was the effect of being in a new place, or perhaps just the effect of being tired, since I had got up so early. But, whatever the explanation, it was a good feeling, and I couldn't help contrasting today with my arrival here nearly

15

four years ago. The day I drove my ambulance through the rain from Salerno into Naples, which had been liberated only a few days before. The weather then had been a personality; something we all hated, and grew to hate even more during that winter of rain and snow and mud. This morning the contrast was so complete that I felt it was a good omen; I believe in such omens.

Luigi's father was home for dinner. I had no clear memory of how he looked, since I had never seen much of him when I had visited the family. But I was a little surprised when he came into the room to greet me. I thought I remembered a much younger man, one of those Italian men in their forties who still exercise and who always look young; instead signor Fabbri is nearly fifty now and he looks at least that. He seems more settled, a little slower than he should be; he is in sharp contrast with the signora, who is chatty and full of life.

At dinner we talked about my trip over: how many days I had been on board, the food, the weather. "Wasn't your mother upset at your leaving?" the signora asked.

"A little bit," I said, "…mostly because the last time I was here there was the war and I came home so sick and tired."

16

"I must write to her and tell her not to worry about you. Oh, but of course, she probably doesn't know Italian and I can't write any English. I'll ask you to write it for me, though."

"I know she would appreciate it."

"Yes, I understand why she would be worried. I know how worried I would be if Luigi went to New York or someplace like that." Signora Fabbri is extremely maternal. Through dinner she badgered Luigi about eating well, not biting his nails (an old habit I recognized like a friend).

"Yes, all mothers are alike," signor Fabbri said.

I suppose in a way that is true, but there seems to be at least a superficial difference between the nervous motherliness of the signora and what I am used to at home.

In the afternoon Luigi and I lay down to rest. For a little while we talked—vaguely, because we were both tired. I felt myself sinking gradually into a kind of daydream, thinking how odd, after all, that I should finally be back in Italy. Through my heavy fatigue I felt a little current of excitement, burning like a pilot-light, because I was here. There is no use trying to deny or to explain away the fact of Italy's fascination for me; I think I remember more events from the six months I was here before than from any other period of my life, and in the three and a half years I was away there was always in me the strong desire to come back. That's probably the main reason for my correspondence with Luigi all this time; he represented a link, my only link really, with Italy. The letters we wrote each other were certainly dull: carefully studied political opinions, news of the theater and new books—nothing of real interest, yet I remembered him as an interesting person. And, after seeing him again now and talking with him briefly, I think I was right.

This evening as we stepped out of the garden of the palazzo for a little walk, I saw that rows of little stands lined the street, displaying strange assortments of torrone—a nougat-like Italian candy—or ten-cent-store American goods: cheap red combs, tiny bottles of bright nail polish, tooth-brushes. All of the stands were elaborately decorated with artificial flowers, colored pictures of Saint Francis, large framed certificates covered with stamps which licensed them to sell; some of them were even illuminated by electric lights.

Luigi explained that it was the feast of Saint Francis, the saint of the little local church up the street and therefore the neighborhood patron. The push-carts were lined up for the festa, which would begin as soon as it grew dark. The street, arched with strings of different-colored electric bulbs, was already filled with very young children, who played like little animals, rolling and pushing one another around on the sidewalk. A large platform had been constructed on the pavement near the entrance to the palazzo.

We walked along the sea toward the center of Naples, almost to Mergellina. The weather was the same, mild as the morning and no colder; there was very little sound—the muted hiss of the water over the sand, the occasional hum of a filobus or the cry of a street vendor. Some of them cried *Ameriiiican,* accenting the last syllable, and I thought they were referring to me until Luigi told me that they were selling American cigarettes. I was relieved that my nationality isn't as obvious as all that, anyway.

When we got back to Posillipo the festa was well under way. The street was jammed with people, so that the infrequent passing cars or busses had to wait long minutes while the crowd pressed itself to the curbs to allow the vehicles to pass. The cigarette sellers seemed to have collected at this point and cries of American filled the air. On the platform a man was auctioning off a large, dead rabbit. "The money is for San Francesco," Luigi said. The auctioneer, an old fisherman whose face was half-hidden by a large

19

white moustache, shouted and jabbered in Neapolitan of which I understood nothing except the frequent references to the saint. While we watched, he completed the sale of the rabbit and held up the next item: two bottles of tomato sauce. By now the electric lights were all shining, although it was still not completely dark, and the various pictures of the saint were all illuminated, either by colored bulbs or by candles.

After that, we came down and had a light supper. Luigi's parents ate at their club. I was tired and have come to bed, where I am writing this. I still can't quite believe that all this has happened today, that less than twenty-four hours ago I was on the ship. As I lie in bed now, so sleepy that the pencil nearly falls from my hand, listening to the slap of the sea against the palazzo, I can almost imagine that I am still on board. I think of last night when we all sat up late on the after-deck, drinking a weak high-ball, and talking idly about Italy; we seemed to be nowhere, in the infinite— Italy seemed as far as ever, improbable, the creation of our imaginations. It almost seems that still, except when occasionally, above the sound of the water, I hear the burst of a firecracker or a distant strain of song to remind me that I have, at long last, come back.

* * *

September, 1947—Sunday.

The last few days I have been busy settling down. Now I have unpacked, changed Traveller's Checks into lire, had my hair cut. The Fabbri's won't hear of my leaving before the end of next month, and I think they really mean the invitation. Naples, the little I've re-seen of it, appears more fascinating, more inexhaustible than ever; my curiosity is unlimited. It's odd perhaps that I should want to stay so long in a city that I have already known, but in the first place I am determined to see nothing in Italy out of a sense of duty, that feeling of having to see it so that when someone at home asks me about it I can be intelligent; and in the second place I know Naples very slightly, in spite of the fact that I spent six months in and out of the city during the war. In those days there was no knowing Naples, really. Not for someone in uniform. All you could see or know was the false Naples that existed for soldiers: the city composed of brothels, bad bars, Army messes and hotels, and officer's clubs, populated by nurses and Waacs and men on leave and men from HQ. The real city, that existed under this surface, lived to itself and either resisted successfully the military life, or was absorbed by it. It was only in the last few weeks of my time here then that I caught a little glimpse of that real city, through my friendship with Luigi and his friends. I think it is more important for me now to see more of that city than to visit the lakes or climb Vesuvius—not that these, too, aren't without value; but there is so much to investigate in Italy, that one has to choose carefully and constantly. The Italy of antiquity, the museums, the galleries—this all interests me, but I am much more interested in the Italy of today, the people that pass in the street on the way to the museum, the man who sells me my newspaper or tries to rob me in the tram.

Already I feel caught up in the rhythm of the Fabbri's daily life. I am almost used to getting up at nine and breakfasting on a tiny cup of coffee with a piece of bread, eating dinner at two-thirty or three in the afternoon and having a light supper at any hour in the evening, from eight on to ten, depending on our activities. I had never realized before how the hours of one's meals change one's life. Here I may still be out, wandering the streets at noon or at one, hours that I am always at table when at home. I feel peculiar still when I look at my watch at twelve-thirty or after and realize that I don't have to hurry home, that I have hours still before eating. And at night it is even stranger to be going to the movies at seven, when I would ordinarily be well along in my dinner, and finding the streets filled with people, shopping, just beginning their evening.

This is all very trivial, but people's lives are composed of these little things: dinner hours, unimportant habits that cement their personalities. And the difference in these little things makes the enormous difference between Italy and America. It is not only the alien language that makes people foreigners.

October 1.

Luigi is thinking of coming to Rome with me. We talked about it this morning while we were lying in our beds waiting for Rosaria, the maid, to finish shining our shoes and bring them back to us. Apparently Luigi has been thinking for some time of leaving Naples, where there seems to be little to occupy him.

Wednesday.

I have really seen very little of Naples, and yet my days seem rather busy. In the morning I always hate to leave until the mail has come and, as a result, my day is always late in beginning. Then, by the time I have walked a bit, or run a few errands (I seem always to have some little thing to do) or accompanied Luigi on errands of his, it is time to have a coffee or a vermouth, rest for a moment, and go home to dinner.

23

But I like these aimless mornings. They are never dull, because for me everything is still new enough to be interesting. I delight in listening to the dreariest of conversations on the bus, for example, just to be putting my Italian to the test. I annoy Luigi occasionally when I insist on looking in all the shop windows—not only the elegant modistes and haber-dashers but also the humblest of stationery shops or delicatessens. The last are especially fascinating with their strange-shaped cheeses suspended on greasy cord or the deep-red salamis. Many of them display choco-late bars and strange sugar-candy, colored and shaped to look like various items of food: fruit or vegetables or even meat. The prospect of eating one of these slabs of sugar fixed up to resemble a slice of roast beef —even to the streaks of fat and the reddish uncooked parts—nauseates me, but I have seen a number of Neapolitan children clutching the stuff in their sticky hands as if it were the best Suchard.

Today as we were walking along the Via Chiaia, we met a girl who was introduced to me only as Rina. Apparently Luigi had talked to her of me, because she seemed to know all about me and asked me all sorts of questions about how long I was going to be in Naples, what I was writing.

She is not a pretty girl, but I found her attractive.

24

Her dark brown hair was cut short, pushed back from her forehead by a narrow brass bandeau. She wore a blouse, sweater, and skirt—all very simple, but in good taste; and she wore these clothes with a casual style. I noticed this as she walked along the street with us—Luigi had asked her where she was going and she had said she would accompany us a bit of the way.

With me, she established herself at once as an Americophile. She handed me a pack of Luckies and asked me in English, "Want a cigarette?" I took one. "These are good; Italian cigarettes are no good."

Luigi immediately began to make fun of her, mimicking her English. "She's crazy," he said, speaking to me in English as if to keep Rina from understanding.

"What you mean crazy?" She pronounced it with a very broad "A". *"You* are a crazy." Then she turned to me and began to talk again in Italian. "This boy thinks he's Benedetto Croce and Mussolini put together."

She apologized afterwards for switching to Italian. "When the American army has been here, I have worked for them for one year. But now I forget everything."

The conversation after that was in Italian, but with occasional English exclamations or interjections from Rina for my benefit. Our remarks seemed to succeed one another without any logic, but in the course of the walk I found out that Rina is engaged to Luigi's uncle Bruno, that she is broke, that she would like to go to America, that she would like a job in Naples with the Consulate or some American business, that she wanted me to write a letter for her in English to a boy in America she knew when he was a soldier here.

She had decided to come out to the palazzo with us and go swimming. It was hot this morning, and the idea of lying on the sand seemed a good one. Rina had no bathing suit with her, but she improvised one, when we got home, out of some shorts of Luigi's and a scarf of mine. I thought how much better she looked, dressed in this haphazard way, than a lot of girls who fuss about such things as bathing suits as if they were Molyneux gowns.

When we were all ready, we descended through the maze-like passages of the palazzo to the beach, which was deserted. For a long time we just lay there taking the sun. Luigi and I said nothing; Rina made piles of sand, then destroyed them, and sang a little, chiefly the same line over and over again, from an American movie that I saw months ago in the States but it is just playing now in Naples. *Put the blame on me, boys,* she sang. And after a pause she would repeat the line.

"It goes 'Put the blame on *Mame,* boys'," I corrected her. "It's a girl's name."

"On Mame," Rina repeated. For a bit she was silent. Then she began singing another song. "Going to *take* a *sen-ti-ment-al* journey…"

Finally we went in swimming. The laziness of being in the sun had enervated me and, after a moment of splashing around in the strangely cold water, I was exhausted. I stumbled to the beach and threw myself down on my back again. Rina and Luigi swam for another few minutes, laughing and calling to each other, occasionally shouting at me to come back. At last Luigi began swimming in earnest, swiftly and neatly, until he had reached some rocks far out from the shore. Rina called after him, then came in and lay beside me, humming "sentimental journey" and digging her toes into the sand. It seemed impossible for her to be absolutely still.

When Luigi had come back, we handed the towel around and dried ourselves, then went in the house. "Ooooo, look at the typewriter," Rina shouted, as soon as she saw it opened on the table in our room. "Now you must write me this letter to my friend in America."

27

I was completely without energy and the last thing I wanted to do was to put myself at the typewriter to work. Noticing this, Luigi said "Another time, Rina." But she was insistent. "Wby another time? Here I am and here is Bill and here is the typewriter." And to me: "Have you got any of that thin paper?"

I took out a sheet of paper and put it in the machine. Rina sat in the easy chair opposite me, dangling her legs over its arm. "Dear George," she began dictating. "Thanks very much for your letter and your Christmas greeting last Christmas. I would have answered them before this, but..."

She paused. "What shall I say, Luigi? I have to think of an excuse. I really *meant* to answer his letter; it was so sweet. But I just never did."

"Why not?" Luigi had taken up a book and was reading. He seemed uninterested both in Rina's letter and the book in front of him.

"Oh you know, I just never had the energy to try to write anything in English. And, of course, he doesn't understand Italian. Isn't that funny; he was right here in Naples for nearly two years and he never learned a word of Italian?" She looked around at us for agreement; Luigi grunted and I nodded.

"Well, say I was sick, Bill, Make it sound as if I really had been."

28

"It's not going to be very convincing, I'm afraid. After all Christmas was nearly ten months ago." I was already fed up with the letter.

"Then say my mother was sick too. Say first I was very, very sick, then after that, my mother was sick." Rina began to get interested in this bit of fiction. "We all thought she was going to die and I have been very busy taking care of her. But she is all right now, at last, thank God, and wants to be remembered to you. She often speaks of you and wonders how you are. I wonder, too, and we both hope you are well."

"Does that sound nice?" Rina asked.

"Now what shall I say?

She reached over and helped herself to one of my Luckies.

"How should I know?" I didn't hide my exasperation, but Rina took no notice.

"Well, I suppose I should ask how his family is," she said, thinking it over. "He has a wife and two children, you know. She must be terrible, though. He told me all about her. He was crazy for me. Ask him how is his family?" She ordered me suddenly.

How is your family? I wrote.

"His wife got terribly sick once while he was over here," Rina went on, "and he told me that, if anything happened to her…but she got well again, of course."

All of this said with the greatest nonchalance, while I waited at the typewriter.

"Now, let's see. Ask him to send us some cigarettes and some soap… By the way, Bill, if you have any soap, I can sell it for you and make you some money."

I told her I didn't have any.

"Well, get someone to send you some. We'll go halves on it and make a lot of money. I could certainly use some money. Did you ask him for the cigarettes? I guess that's all, then."

Somehow or other, we finished off the letter. Rina signed it and I put it hastily in an envelope, not daring to reread it.

"I don't suppose you have a stamp?"

I didn't.

"That's all right." She tucked the letter carelessly into her jammed purse, and I had a feeling that it would never be mailed; all my work for nothing.

Rina leaned back in the chair, blowing the smoke from her cigarette up into the air, watching it dispersed by the sea-breeze from the window. "America," she mused. "How I wish I could go there. Bruno and I want so much to emigrate. He had a wonderful idea.

Now listen to this, Luigi." He had, with his usual casualness, continued reading. "We thought we'd open up an Italian restaurant. With all those Italians in America, we'd certainly make a lot of money."

I thought of the Italian restaurant in town at home that had failed shortly before I left. "I don't know," I remarked cautiously, not wanting to destroy a favorite daydream. "There are already many Italian restaurants in America, and not all of them make money, you know."

"Oh, but ours would be different." She was not in the least disturbed by my pessimism. "We would have real Neapolitan cooking. Bruno and I would supervise everything. The waiters would all be dressed as fishermen or something like that, and we'd call it *Napoli*..."

I saw that it was foolish of me to consider all this seriously. Why was I allowing myself to worry about the success of this mythical restaurant? Rina would never go to America, the *Napoli* would never exist... and yet I felt myself concerned about it all.

At this point Signora Fabbri came home. She was a little surprised—and I thought, displeased—to see Rina there, but they greeted each other very affectionately. Rina chatted on for a while, telling us the story of a movie she had seen the night before,

31

then she changed her clothes and left, thanking me
for the use of my scarf, which she threw, still damp,
on my pillow.

Pazza, the Signora said, when Rina had left.
"Crazy." And she touched her temple with her forefin-
ger and rolled her eyes imitating a lunatic.

After we had eaten, Luigi told me most of the
story of Rina. She is Bruno's mistress, it seems, and
for this Signora Fabbri doesn't entirely approve.

"But isn't she somewhat younger than your
uncle?" I asked.

"About ten years," he answered. "But she is in
love with him and it doesn't matter to her."

"I should think she'd be more the age for you
than for your uncle," I said, joking.

"We used to be lovers, as a matter of fact, but
she really prefers Bruno." He said this very calmly, as
if it were the most natural thing in the world.

"But don't you find it a little embarrassing now?"

"Why?" He was surprised at my question. "Bruno
is satisfied and Rina is satisfied, and so am I. What is
there to bother anybody then?"

"Nothing, I suppose." Then I said, half to myself,
"Rina must really be a little crazy."

"She is. Her mother is in a sanitarium half the
time, when they can afford it. Poor Rina. And her

32

father was killed in Ethiopia, but everyone says that he was a little bit…too."

"Doesn't Bruno mind this somehow?"

"He's crazy, too," Luigi said. Then he elaborated. "You know, I think almost everyone in Naples is a little insane. Rina is crazy, my brother is crazy, Rosaria is crazy, I most certainly am crazy. My father, perhaps, is the only sane one; but sometimes I think that his very normalcy is a form of madness."

"But what if Bruno and Rina are married and have children…?"

"Why, they'll never be married. Bruno isn't going to marry Rina."

"Doesn't he love her?" The whole situation was becoming more and more incomprehensible to me.

"He's fond of her, I suppose, in his way. But he couldn't possibly marry her. He doesn't have any money, for one thing, and the family would never approve." Luigi spoke as if the whole thing had been explained.

Saturday.

Gradually I am beginning to realize what a change has taken place in Luigi in the three and a half years since I saw him last. At first I thought he was almost the same; in fact, I was a little surprised that he seemed so slightly affected by the passage of time

33

which has transformed me completely. But now that I have been here two weeks (is it that long already?), I begin to realize that he too is very different from the boy he was in those days during the war.

It is not so much any physical difference. Perhaps he is a little thinner and, perhaps, a little less strikingly good-looking. His eyes seem just a shade less bright, and his walk just a bit languorous. But all these are very slight; they may be things that I see now, after I have thought of the other things, the inner and more important changes.

It is almost as if there were a dead weight inside him, something that oppresses him. At first it seemed just plain laziness—his unwillingness to stir himself for certain things, his lack of interest in plans of his family for visiting people or taking me places to show me things. But it is more than that: he seems to be unable to get concerned about anything. If we start discussing a writer or a belief on which we differ, he does not enter into the argument, but rather fondles his own point of view, then abandons it if it seems untenable. Frequently I find myself beginning a discussion with him and then suddenly I realize that the argument is over and I have won, without having had to fight at all. It's like a huge army's preparing to attack a town, marching in with their weapons ready, silencing their footsteps, only to find that the town is deserted, the enemy has already conceded it; and the victory that they expected turns out to be nothing, an illusion.

I suppose I am unusually concerned about Luigi, but the change is really incredible. I keep thinking of the time when I was here before. In those days he seemed to live only in his mental life. Athlete, sportsman that he was, his only real excitement came then from the pursuit of an idea, the trapping of a false opinion and exposing it. I recall now the sessions we used to have, talking at each other in my dreadful Italian of those days, his passable English, and the mediocre French that both of us could muster in the pinches. Now I wonder how we found so much to talk about. And all of it seemed so vital, so important. The scenes come flooding back to me: Luigi running into my room with a half-done translation of Eliot or Sherwood Anderson or (alas) Saroyan and asking me to explain the significance of "yew tree," or "screen door" or "little people," and how seriously I took everything, being quite careful to give exactly the nuance I thought was intended. Other times Luigi would come with friends and they would read me what they had written: poetry, stories, essays, criticism. And they would translate all the longer words until I had only the vaguest idea of what the whole thing meant, but I got the idea that they were at least stirred up about writing, that they meant to do something, and that stirred me up as well. And the least thing I wrote became for them a kind of Rosetta stone, to be studied, deciphered, and handled with respect.

"You can't imagine what it is that we feel," Peppino had said one day. "It's as if we had been all of our lives in prison and paper and pen had been forbidden us. Now we are out in the air again and we want to write all the things we have been saving up all this time."

And I thought then that a lifetime didn't seem long enough for them. They were writing so furiously that it was as if they had only a few days to get it all said in. Luigi then seemed to be the most active of all, the most interested in everything: he translated for the others, most of whom knew no English, he wrote for the radio station that the army had set up, he started a magazine when they had barely enough money to buy the paper for one issue and pay the printer and yet it survived for several months—the issues came to me in America full of their things, appreciations of Auden and Rex Warner and Dylan Thomas and—to my horror—translations of some of my bad poetry that I had written here in Naples and left with them.

Monday.

My occasional, very occasional, homesickness manifests itself in little ways. For instance, this morning when I used the last of my Colgate's tooth-paste. As I was about to throw away the flat, squeezed-out tube, an irrational impulse suggested that I keep it as some kind of meaningless souvenir. For a moment I hesitated, almost put it back in my toilet-kit, then I tossed the useless thing in the waste-basket. As I did so, it seemed to me that I was cutting another one of the numberless ties that link me with America. I suddenly remembered clearly the day I had bought the tooth-paste, one morning when I went into Shiner's Drug Store and bought a lot of supplies for my trip: tooth-paste, razor blades, soap. All of them used up now.

I don't think I felt any real desire to be back in Virginia, or to be any place other than Naples; but I did feel, all at once, solitary and distant.

Later in the day I went into the city and at the pharmacy in Piazza S. Ferdinando, I bought a tube of Kolynos made in Italy. Crema per i Denti. It looks odd and foreign. I put the tube on the table in the bathroom. Luigi has one exactly like it.

★　★　★

Tuesday.

I decided the other day that I should spend one of the next clear mornings doing a special kind of sightseeing: i.e., looking again at those places that were most familiar to me during the war, the improvised landmarks of Naples in 1943-44. Yesterday it rained and I stayed in the house nearly all day reading. Finally today, after I had had my coffee and shaved, I explained to Luigi that I was going out, and left.

It was a foolish project. I really knew in advance what I would find, the changes that would have occurred. And yet, it was something I felt I had to do, a responsibility toward myself. Never afterward would I be able to tell someone about having seen these places—they were significant only to me and to perhaps a handful of wartime friends of mine, all in America naturally, forgetting the war.

I got off the number 40 bus in Piazza Plebiscito, walked past the royal palace, down the steps to the long street that runs along the port, where the various docks are, including the Maritime Station, where my ship landed two weeks ago. The traffic here was very heavy; a continuous cloud of white dust hung over everything: the trucks that rattled by, the donkey-carts, myself. Heavy wire fenced off the actual dock areas from the street, and the various entrances were guarded by sailors. A little of the wartime atmosphere remains there—perhaps there more than other places in Naples—but the sailors are Italian, and a little shabby, and they joke with the passers-by and do not stand always strictly at attention.

Of course, I remembered the old days, the times when our ambulances crowded the quays, loading the wounded onto hospital ships, or the day when I myself finally rode out in the lighter to the Liberty ship that took me and sixteen others home. And finally, after I had walked almost to the end of the area, to the point where the buildings thin out and the street becomes the road to Castellammare, there I recalled the evening I had thought I would never forget.

It wasn't anything really very important. But it was under a certain portico in the dock area (I found it quite easily this morning) that I had stood once for an hour or so during a German air raid on the port. A very small raid, but it was the first I had been in, and I had been rather frightened, standing in the doorway with three or four English soldiers, to whom the whole thing was old stuff, and who talked to me, as to one of themselves, with ease, joking about the flares, the attack, and the occasional near one that shook plaster from the wall down over us like snow.

I thought of this today and realized how much I had forgotten, how dim most of the details were in my mind. How easily you forget these things. At the time—and for a long while afterward—that evening seemed the most important of my life; I thought I would always be able to feel it all again, merely by thinking of it. And yet, this morning, standing again in that very doorway, I found that it was impossible to recapture really that fright, or anxiety, or the relief that followed when I stepped out into the dusty evening to find my ambulance untouched and I shook hands with the Tommies and drove off to the hospital in Castellammare where I was stationed.

I think it is in his "Cape Cod" that Thoreau says something to the effect that, "We can never remember the sublime moments, we remember only how we itched or our feet hurt..." One remembers the moments, perhaps, but cannot re-feel them.

Quickly I retraced my steps, passing the palace again, until I got to the Gallery. It, too, retains some of that equivocal, war-time appearance that Burns recreated so beautifully in his novel about Naples. The glass has been put back in the arcade's roof now; but it leaks, and this morning there was a large puddle at the center, where the two arms of the gallery cross, a leftover from yesterday's rain. I sat down at one of the cafes and ordered a vermouth and there I remembered the first time I saw the Gallery, when we had driven into Naples a few days after its liberation (or after the American occupation, as they say here now) and we parked in the square outside and a group of us came running into this peculiar building and saw that there was a bar open. We ordered champagne, I remember, and the Neapolitans hadn't yet realized the extent of their inflation, so they charged us only 70 cents a bottle for it. We must have had at least a bottle apiece before we got back into our cars and drove up the hill to the hospital that we were supposed to open and work in.

I didn't bother to ask the waiter what champagne cost now. The price had begun to rise after our debauch that afternoon and I dare say it's rising still. It took the Neapolitans a very short time to catch on to the business of inflation and the occupation currency, which is still in circulation now, another little souvenir of the past.

After I had paid for my vermouth (the former price of the champagne just about), I went out and began walking up the Via Roma until I got to the Museum, then I turned left and started the ascent into the Vomero section of Naples. It is quite a long walk;

but after I had reached a certain height, I could stop from time to time at parapets that look down over the city. I rested frequently and watched the activity of Naples below me. After the docks and the Gallery, I still had in my mind the idea of what the city had been like before; and I kept feeling that it was too quiet this morning. I thought perhaps there should be more trucks, some jeeps, an occasional ambulance. I don't think I would have been surprised if a lot of olive-drab vehicles had suddenly appeared; to me that traffic is such a part of the Naples I first knew that it seems almost a permanent thing.

But nothing of the sort happened. The traffic remained what it was: many Fiats, a rare American car, a battered truck that may once have been G.I. but had long since lost its characteristic color and become the grey of the dust it was covered with. Naples this morning was a city at peace: the trams clattered past me as I walked up Via Tasso, the maids shook cloths out of the windows, children played the Italian variety of hopscotch, which I have often watched but never understood.

I was looking for a particular house: number 615. During the war it was the club-house and rest-center for our ambulance group. I spent a number of leaves there; and later, when I was living down in the

42

Fabbri's palazzo, I used to go up to Via Tasso to get my mail, see my friends.

The house was unusual and very easily recognized. It sat above me as I walked up the hill: a kind of false Gothic building, pretentious and ugly, built in the 1920's. I saw all the familiar outlines: the weird tower that made a little angle in the main living-room, the strange-shaped windows of the stairway, the peculiar terrace off the writing-room upstairs. As soon at I got near the house I noticed that all the windows were open, but none of them appeared to have any curtains. It was hard to tell if the place was empty or not. It was supposed to be jinxed: our group had inherited it from a prominent Fascist who fled Naples and later killed himself; he had bought it from the builder, who had gone bankrupt building it. And this morning the place had a kind of haunted air about it; I thought the windows might be opened to drive out the evil memories.

Among which I am sure there would be the famous night that Bill and Vance and Andy and I got drunk. For no reason at all, or at least for no very specific one, we started drinking one evening. Each of us had a bottle of some kind, and we began quietly, pouring a bit of whatever it was into a glass, gulping it down, and then pouring in some more. After a while, we started offering the others what we were drinking and accepting a bit out of their bottles in return. And gradually, the whole room began fading away with us and we found ourselves isolated in a magnificent hilarity. Everything anyone said, any gesture was indescribably funny; we roared. We sang. Finally at one point one of us—Vance, I think—began to make up a parody of one of the Negro spirituals we had been singing.

The words of the parody came back to me this morning—after these years—they seemed to come roaring out of the open windows of the house:

"Were you there when they nailed him to the cross?
Were you there when they nailed him to the cross?
Did he holler, did he beller?
Was he brave, or was he yeller?
Were you there when they crucified my Lord?"

How we laughed. The tears started in our eyes; we ached. We complained of aching, but laughed all the more. Finally, when we had calmed ourselves to a reasonable degree, Bill had made up another verse that had to be listened to.

"Were you there when they raffled off his clothes?
Were you there when they raffled off his clothes?
Did you play that game of chance
For the Lord my Savior's pants?
Were you there when they crucified my Lord?"

44

And again we were laughing, and so on and on until it was suddenly very late and we went off to bed, the evening already becoming a memory. It seemed to us the next morning that we had never been so drunk, that we had never laughed so hard or heard things so killingly funny.

Today I couldn't help thinking how young we all were then, how terribly far away all that time is. Vance now a newspaperman; Bill expecting his first child; Andy in a monastery. And I…here I am. As I stood in front of the house, listening to those memories, I thought that I couldn't remember having been drunk like that or laughed like that since the war. And I can't remember having been frightened again as I was that night in the docks. Does this mean that I never will experience things that strongly again? Is it possible that the war was the significant experience of my life, that all the time I was drinking and laughing, I was living more fully, more deeply, than I ever will again? Now I seem very conscious of every emotion I feel, and for that I seem to feel things less deeply. And I think this is a bit of what I have begun to notice in Luigi, a frightening self-consciousness, an introspection that renders him inactive and unfeeling.

On the other hand, I am not sure that I would want to return to that wartime stage in my emotional development. It may be that I am better off as I am. This was impressed on me later on this morning, after I left the house on Via Tasso, turned off into the alley behind it, that leads across the Vomero to the street that ascends further, to the top of the hill. There I came again to the Ospedale Ventitre Marzo, which Mussolini built, large and imposing, another landmark of my war months.

In my day it was called the 92nd General Hospital and I used to bring patients there up from Castellammare, and later down from Caserta and the Garigliano. It is civilian again now and there are no guards at the gates, no soldiers lounging about the grounds, or carrying their mess-tins, no nurses calling to one another in English, and none of the familiar Dodge ambulances. There is only one reminder of the old days: the large American Army cemetery in the broad field to the right of the main building of the hospital.

I walked over there and saw the files of white crosses, the grass neatly cut, the names neatly painted. I walked along a few rows and looked at the names, all of them unfamiliar. I know really one person buried there, and I don't know his name.

He's an American boy who died in my ambulance, the victim of a foolish accident. He was in the

hold of a ship in the harbor of Castellammare, han-
dling an unloading crew; and through the carelessness
of one of the workers on deck, a huge six-by-six
beam fell down on him and crushed him. I took my
ambulance down there as soon as they called, but the
boy was dying and I knew he was dead when I helped
lift the stretcher into place. Another soldier, the dead
boy's friend, sat on the ground at the back of the
machine, crying and talking to the boy as if he were
alive. When I drove away the soldier was still sitting
there; the others stood awkwardly around him, not
knowing what to do.

I didn't know what to do either; I had always got
my patients to the hospital alive before. And during
the long drive over the rough, pitted road, I tried to
think what I was supposed to do. I was sure that the
army had all sorts of forms and routines to cover such
a death, but I was unfamiliar with them and I dreaded
the monstrous red tape. And more than that, I was
rigorously trying to prevent myself from thinking of
the dead boy in the back, of the crushed face I had
caught a glimpse of before the blanket covered it, of
the bloody board they had carried him to me on.

Finally I got to the hospital and began to go
through the ritual of filling out the death certificate.
First the doctor came to my ambulance and looked at

47

the boy, then I had to leave the ambulance (which I did reluctantly for some reason) and go inside to the office, where I had to answer questions, sign things, until at last the doctor said, "Now you can take the body over to be buried."

I had never taken a body to be buried before but I didn't feel like asking for further instructions from the medical officer, so I went back to my car and drove it over to the broad field, which had just been turned into a cemetery. There was a short line of graves (nothing like the vast extent today) and a few tents where the burial squad lived and had an office.

They went about their work very effectively. I had nothing to do except watch them, as they ripped off the blanket and threw it on the floor of the ambulance, took off one dog-tag and left another, put the soldier's watch and wallet and a few other objects in a little bag. There were also two packs of Camels in the boy's pocket. "No use in sending these to his mother," one of the burial men said, and tossed them into the ambulance where they had thrown the blanket.

And finally they lifted the body off the stretcher. His broken limbs swung the wrong way as they shook the corpse into a bag and carried it off to an open grave, already dug, waiting at the end of the row of crosses.

After that I went out to lunch with a nurse I had been seeing something of at the hospital in Naples, always thinking that perhaps she might be available (my friends had assured me she was), And I thought I liked her, because she was stupid and frankly sensual and, I thought, healthy. But at lunch that day I didn't feel like talking to her. When she noticed how quiet I was, she asked what was wrong and I told her a boy had died in my ambulance.

"Was he young?" she asked at once.

I said he was.

"Was he attractive?"

I could understand that the question was automatic; but the obvious sexual interest that was behind it, the whole physical preoccupation of the girl, jolted me, nauseated me. Not for herself so much, but because I was suddenly aware of all my own little designs, the thought I had had of what this lunch should lead to, and what would happen after that. All my nervous, hopeful calculations suddenly seemed false and disgusting.

After that I don't think I saw her more than once or twice by chance around the hospital. Later I found another nurse, when I had forgotten my scruples: and, not long after that, one day when cigarettes were scarce, I smoked the Camels that had been in the dead man's pocket.

I looked along the first row of crosses, trying to figure out which might mark the grave of that young boy. Was he Pvt. Kenneth Adams, or Pfc. Henry Forsythe, or Cpl. Edgar Brown? The nurses' names, too, I had forgotten; I couldn't even remember what they looked like.

Suddenly some bells tolled and I looked at my watch. It was half past twelve and time I was getting home. I managed to find a tram that went down as far as Piazza dei Martiri, and I took the bus from there. But it was a long and slow ride; I was nearly late for dinner.

Luigi asked me where I had been.

"I went to the Ospedale Ventitre Marzo and some other places I used to see a lot during the war," I said.

"What did you want to go and look at them for?"

I didn't know how to answer him.

Thursday.

These mornings lately I have acquired the habit of stopping by Middleton's Tearoom on the Via Caracciolo on my way home to dinner. It's very pleasant there about twelve-thirty or one; and I enjoy myself, sitting with a vermouth in front of me, the sun (which is amazingly warm still) beating on my face.

50

It is impossible to read in that glare, so I lie back in my chair with my eyes closed and let my mind wander. Then there occurs a strange phenomenon that I had noticed before: that frequently a particular place becomes associated in one's mind with a particular train of thought. I remember at college how for months I would automatically begin whistling a certain air of Mozart's when I walked down the corridor that led to my rooms—for no reason at all. Finally I became conscious of this repetition and it stopped.

So this morning I realized that these last few days my thoughts have been running always in the same direction during my drowsy moments at Middleton's. I seem to have been thinking chiefly about home — why, I don't know. Perhaps it is because of the sea, which stretches out so apparently infinite, that one cannot help but entertain the old trite thoughts about how far away New York is, one wonders what the time is there, what the weather's like.

And, of course, I imagine all my friends going about their regular occupations. It pleases me somehow to think that if I went back tomorrow after these weeks so completely removed, so different, I would still know exactly the right subway to take, the right phone numbers to call. I enjoy this knowledge that, back in New York, there exists this complicated machinery of city life that I comprehend and can use. Because Naples, in spite of my progress, remains always a foreign place, where I can imagine a host of perfectly ordinary situations in which I would be at a complete loss.

This thought leads me so believe also that it would really be impossible for me ever to absorb this way of life here completely. Not for any mystical reason, but simply because it has too much of a head start on me. There are too many details that I would never have time to learn. I agree with Henry James that a writer needs the background of an older culture, an established way of life; but it seems to me that by choosing England, he took the easiest way out. He had the advantage of a common language and, in a certain sense, a common heritage; America, in spite of everything, remains a cultural continuation of England.

For myself, then, I think that I shall continue to get as far into Italy as I can. But sooner or later, I know that I will go home, where this machine of daily life is a time-saving device that one uses, not a work of art that one spends his time studying.

I thought over all this today, recalling New York quite clearly as I did, thinking of those last days there, the very conscious "last" dinner at La Geule, the last movie, the last drink, the last party, the last kiss. That long series of little things that were made events by the imminence of my going away. I was beginning to feel just a little sentimental about these things when Luigi came up.

"Are you sleeping?" he asked.

I opened my eyes. "No, just wasting time."

He sat down and ordered a vermouth. "I've just had a kind of adventure."

I asked him what it was and he explained to me. He had just met a girl and made an appointment with her.

"What sort of girl was she? A whore?"

"Not exactly." Luigi was interested himself in analyzing her. "I imagine she works sometimes as a whore, but she doesn't have the looks of one. She is the daughter of a fisherman I know—he keeps his boat near the house and I've been out fishing with him several times. She's rather pretty, very healthy-looking, fresh, still quite young—under twenty, at any rate—and with none of that air of being spoiled or commercialized. No, not at all like a whore, more like a fisherman's daughter gone wrong, if you see what I mean. An attractive idea, somehow."

He went on dissecting the appearance and the attraction of the girl in this way, half aesthetically and half sensually. Something in his tone, a kind of superi-

53

ority or inhumanity, annoyed me and I interrupted him, a little sharply.

"For some reason, the whole idea of this appointment, the coldness and the unfeelingness of it, revolts me. I suppose that, at heart, I'm really an American Puritan."

"So am I really," Luigi said at once. "I am very much a Puritan. I am not really very sensual at all. You may not think it, but sometimes I can go for as long as two weeks, even more, without...anything."

I couldn't help laughing at Luigi's idea of a Puritan: one who can go without sex for two weeks. I had to explain to him why I had laughed, and when I did, he laughed too, but I'm afraid he didn't quite understand even then.

It was late and we got up to go home. We walked—the weather was so perfect—following the sea, through the Villa Nazionale, past Mergellina, where the fishermen were spreading their nets.

"It's such a fine day," Luigi said, "we ought to go out in a boat this afternoon."

"Wonderful," I agreed.

"We could hire one very easily from one of the men near the house and we could go out into the bay, perhaps to Marechiaro or to Nisida—you've never been to Nisida. We could perhaps even take our bathing suits if it stays warm and sunny like this. Or we could take a little something to eat and stay out until dark."

He went on, enlarging his idea and fantasticating until our little trip out in the boat had become something like Columbus' expedition. I realized very quickly that we wouldn't go, that he would amuse himself by picturing the trip in all its varied, rich possibility until finally he would be bored with the idea and this afternoon, after dinner, he would have forgotten all about it, we would eat, then lie down to rest as usual, then get up and go to a movie or to the club.

I remembered then that we had said something to Rina about going to a movie this evening and I thought that perhaps Luigi's assignation might interfere.

"When is your appointment with the fisherman's daughter?" I asked him.

"Oh, it isn't anything definite, really. She just told me where I could find her any evening at a particular hour and told me to come whenever I wanted." He said this without any interest; he was still thinking of our boat trip. And I knew then that he would not see this girl again probably, any more than we would spend the afternoon on the bay.

*   *   *

55

Tuesday.

For me, looking at Naples these days is like reading one of those ancient manuscripts which has been written over several times, so that the various stories, old and new, interlace and confound one another. Or like looking at Troy, a city composed of intermingling levels, more modern or more ancient.

I see always, of course, the present city, the living people who walk past me on their own errands, who touch me in busses, whose voices make up the loud forest of sound that is overlaid upon the city. But then I look at these men and women more closely, and they seem to belong to all epochs: a beggar dressed in the tatters of a British uniform, or a servant out shopping in a coat obviously cut down from a US army overcoat, reminds me that only a short while back the city had a different orientation. And when, once in a while, I see one of the boys selling black market cigarettes dressed in an Italian soldier's military grey, I remember the effect that those unkempt uniforms had on me when I was first in Italy. When I saw them, the soldiers who had deserted the army and had no clothes to change to, I thought that I was seeing Defeat, symbolized in those clothes and expressed in those faces.

The air of Defeat hangs over the city in spite of everything, in spite of the newly made buildings, in spite of the posters celebrating Rita Hayworth and Clark Gable. There it is in the very faces of the cigarette-sellers, in the nervous way the children run to pick up butts which they sell later by the kilo to be made into fake Luckies or Camels or Chesterfields.

There are times now when I feel really a conqueror—a sensation I never had before when I was slouching around in a nondescript battledress, only slightly more presentable than those of the beggars and refugees. But now, as I walk around, I see everywhere the lasting effects of the American occupation. Even the language has felt the influence: several times I have heard two Italians greet each other with "hey, Joe," and the word "signoreen"—the American mispronunciation of *signorina* has become in Naples a synonym for whore.

Tuesday.

Tomorrow Luigi and I are going to Capri. Not exactly for pleasure, but with something like a mission: to get Luigi's younger brother, Cesare, to come home.

Cesare I remember very slightly. When I was here before he was sixteen or seventeen; he was strikingly good looking then, I remember—it was the first and most lasting thing one noticed about him. I also recall that he spoke Neapolitan almost exclusively, to the annoyance of his parents; and had been in jail under the Fascists because he had led a student demonstration against the war.

When I arrived last week I asked about him, and Luigi only said rather vaguely, "Yes, he's very well. He's at Capri now."

This morning Luigi had apparently a long discussion with his parents while I was out, because after dinner this afternoon he suggested the trip to Capri.

"Fine," I said.

"I have to go," he explained, "to get Cesare. So we won't stay very long this time. I'm just supposed to get him and bring him back. We may just remain one day, or at most overnight."

"All right," I agreed. Somehow it struck me that there was some mystery about the trip, about Cesare's stay at Capri. "What is he doing out there, by the way?" Naively, I assumed that he must have some job.

Luigi sighed. "Dear Bill, my brother is ruining the family. That is why my father is sending me there to bring him home. My father is so good, you can't realize. Cesare has run up tremendous debts; my father has had to borrow a great deal of money, and in these times...well, things have not been as before.

58

You must have noticed how my father has aged; he has had such a hard time, and now Cesare…"

"But what does he do on Capri?" Never having been to Capri, I could imagine only a pretty island with a beach. I could not picture anyone staying there indefinitely, without some kind of occupation, or at least the excuse of one.

"Well, he is very amusing and good-looking and people like to have him around them." Luigi didn't exactly understand my question, I'm afraid, and I didn't know how to make myself clearer. Luigi felt that his answer had explained everything, and I let it go at that.

In any case, I will see for myself tomorrow. Finally Capri. During the war I never managed to get there; the Air Force had requisitioned it. That, and Sorrento and Lake Como and, I suppose, Florence, are the places people like Aunt H. always mention about Italy, along with the Champs Elysées, Notre Dame, Lake Louise and Banff.

I am very curious and excited. We will get up early and take the boat that leaves downtown at seven a.m.

Friday.

Back from Capri last night. It seems incredible that everything happened in two days—less than two days, in fact. I seem to have met enough people, had enough experiences, to last months. I did nothing but talk. Luigi acted as a chorus, explaining others to me and me to others, commenting on the scenery, calling my attention to details that otherwise would have escaped my notice.

Cesare was, naturally, the center of everything. I was a little dubious of our finding him easily. I knew Capri is a small place; but even in a village a person can be difficult to track down. On the boat going out I asked Luigi how we would find him.

"Oh, he'll be in the square, no doubt, by the time we get there. It may be just a little early, but in any case, he'll be there by ten." Luigi seemed perfectly assured of this, so I let it go. It wasn't my look-out; I was just being taken along for company.

It was after nine when we finally got to the island. The file of passengers flowed off the boat and was swallowed up immediately in a swarm of touts, porters from hotels, taxi-drivers, all ready to fall on the unwary and pick them clean. Luigi led me through the mob into the clear.

We rode the flimsy funicular up the hill to the town, creaking through beautifully fertile little gardens, filled with orange and lemon trees, past lovely miniature villas, all plaster and tile, beautifully neat and airy. At last we arrived at the upper end of the line and got out, again to fight through the collection of touts, until we got into the main square of the town.

It *is* beautiful. Instinctively I have always wanted to deprecate Capri, partly in defiance of Aunt H. and all the other tourists who had talked to me about it. But the square, the first thing I had a settled look at, showed me that I couldn't detract from Capri's real beauty, no matter how hard I tried. There is nothing to do but give in to that strange arrangement of broad steps, narrow arches, slanting streets that lead away toward the other side of the island.

"There's Cesare," Luigi said, waving.

He was sitting at a table in front of the cafe at the far end of the square. It was still rather early for Capri, so the other tables—there was a whole army of them through the square—were largely deserted. He waved at us languidly, but did not get up to come and meet us.

"You remember Bill." Luigi had shaken hands with his brother. Then I did.

"Yes, of course. I thought you'd be coming back," he said. "America must be intolerable this time of year." He was smiling and I smiled back, trying really to recognize this boy as the one I had known before.

He has changed completely; even his face seems

61

quite different. It is heavy, almost vulgar, and entirely mature. His body, too, has none of the youthfulness that it had before. Still he is good-looking, or rather he is attractive: very well-developed, strong-looking, brown—but with always just a suggestion of weakness, more in his way of carrying himself, than in any physical feature. Yesterday morning he was dressed in typically Capri fashion: a pink shirt of some rough material, open at the neck, corduroy pants, leather sandals.

With a great gesture he invited us to have something, calling the waiter over by name, suggesting the chocolate with whipped cream, which Luigi and I both ordered. Then he lapsed back in his half-reclining position in the chair so that he looked, with the slight curl of his lip and the heavy lidded eyes, like some dissolute Roman.

"What brings you pair of intellectuals to this frivolous spot?" he asked finally, when we were starting our chocolate.

I had been waiting for that question, wondering how Luigi would be able to work up to the right answer, tactfully suggest Cesare's coming home.

"Father wants you to come home. I've been sent out to get you." Luigi was smiling as he said this. Cesare immediately burst out laughing, and Luigi's smile broadened until he was laughing, too. What had seemed so serious to him the other afternoon in Naples had now become a kind of joke.

"And I suppose you brought Bill along for protection." They both laughed again.

I would have liked to join in their hilarity, but I kept thinking of the terrible picture Luigi had painted for me of family ruin. Could he have been only exaggerating? But I remembered also the look of Signor Fabbri. The situation was serious; the laughter of Cesare I could almost expect—he was supposed, after all, to be a heartless spendthrift wastrel—but I did not see how Luigi could join in. He should have played the part of the stern and serious, responsible member of the family. I imagined myself in his shoes, gone to—where? Miami? Newport? Bermuda?—to retrieve an erring brother, how impressed I would be with my own position. how determined not to succumb to the vain pleasures of the sinner. Here we were drinking chocolate, the table rocking with their laughter.

Cesare agreed immediately to come home. "But I can't possibly come this afternoon—tomorrow afternoon will be soon enough. Besides there's no point in your rushing away now that you're here. Bill should be shown Capri, too—think of your duties as a

63

host. There're are all sorts of people here he'd be interested to meet." He went on to name several prominent writers and painters, Italian and others.

The idea of staying overnight found prompt acceptance in Luigi. "But absolutely tomorrow. You can't make any excuses then. You understand."

"Of course, of course."

Luigi couldn't continue in this sudden vein of authority, because Cesare had suddenly been surrounded by a group of friends. He introduced us all around, but very lackadaisically so that nobody caught anyone's name. The others sat down and ordered chocolates, so I had an opportunity to look them over.

There were four of them. One a young Italian, perhaps twenty-eight, athletic and rather stupid-looking, very voluble. A girl, about the same age, apparently English, blonde and a little hard, who spoke only bad French to Cesare, when she did speak, which wasn't much.

The other woman, dark and strange and older than the others, left us after a moment, when she was waved to from another table. The fourth an Englishman, very fat, brown without being healthy, apparently in the company of the blonde girl. He spoke no Italian obviously and extremely poor French, but showed no desire to converse with me, although I experienced for just a moment that inclination to speak English that one feels on meeting a fellow Anglosaxon—even the most unattractive one—in a group where one has been speaking a foreign language.

At any rate, it became apparent after a bit that we were a group. When the new arrivals had finished their chocolate, we piled into a taxi and wound down the serpentine road to the *Marina Piccola*. Somebody, I think the Englishman, paid off the driver and we went to the bath-houses to change. Luigi and I had brought no luggage except our bathing-suits wrapped in towels. We put these on and went out on the sand.

There ensued the long discussion about which to do first: sun or bathe. Finally we all pushed out into the water. It is beautifully clear, like crystal, and was pleasantly warm. There were a number of people in bathing, some with inflated rubber contraptions that they floated about on; others paddled little kayak-like affairs. From the water I looked at the beach; people were spread out along it in irregular rows like clothes stretched out to dry. Luigi tells me, though, that in the warmer months it is five or six times as crowded.

I soon came out of the water and lay on the sand, nearly falling asleep—I had got up so early. At last the others found me and produced from somewhere a cold bottle of white wine, which passed from one to the other. It tasted wonderful, and I drank more than I should have. I felt drunk right away.

People wandered past us, sometimes, stepping over our legs or just missing our heads. Once in a while a voice said hello, or bon jour, or ciao.

The English girl (whom I was calling Jane by that time) was next to me; occasionally she would identify these passers-by. Once she answered back, "Ciao, Alberto. Then to me. "That's M—, you know, the novelist.

I knew M—'s work very well. He is one of the most prominent younger writers in Italy—"younger" in that he's about forty and began getting known in the late twenties about the same time that Hemingway and the "younger" American writers acquired their names. M—'s work is quite different from theirs, however; he writes novels of the bourgeoisie with a kind of cold bitter dryness that makes him a sociologist of the middle class that real sociologists generally ignore for the more interesting poor. I was a little surprised to see him at Capri—the equivalent of seeing Steinbeck in the Stork Club—but I thought no more about it at the time, lapsed back into my sun-and-wine induced dozing.

Finally we moved toward lunch. Luigi and I went back and changed our clothes. Others ate in various costume: Cesare put his pink shirt on, Jane found a kind of dressing-gown, the Englishman (Henry) and the Italian (his name is Ollieri, but the others call him O'Leary and make a joke about his being Irish) wore just their bathing-suits and spattered spaghetti-sauce over their bare chests.

We ate in one of the outdoor restaurants right on the beach, under a pergola, covered with vines, pleasant and cool. The place was filled without seeming crowded, and I could look around and see the curious variety of the shifting population of Capri: Swedes, Swiss, Americans, a few English, and a few Italians, who tried to make themselves as American-looking as possible. All were dressed (up to a point) in that wild assortment of bright colors and exotic materials that for its bizarre-ness is unmatched anywhere. I'm sure that even in Hollywood, one couldn't wear some of the things that are commonplace on the island.

When we had finished the spaghetti and were discussing idly the next course, M— and his wife appeared. Jane, who was presiding at the head of the table, summoned them over. "Alberto," she called, using the tone that she might use for a waiter. She made them sit at the table, patronizing them so shamelessly that I was embarrassed. M— took it all with complete equanimity. He was sitting opposite me and, while Jane poured wine in his glass as if she were dispensing alms, he opened a conversation with me.

First we talked in English—he has lived in New York and London and knows them both well—then gradually we lapsed into Italian. We conversed a while about his books, their translations into English, his American publishers. We found we had some mutual acquaintances in America. Finally he asked me how I liked Capri.

"It's very beautiful, of course," I answered, "but I don't think I could do any work here. It seems to me rather enervating."

"It's your digestion," he said at once. "You have to get accustomed to the air here. I was sick for a month when I first came. But now I work a great deal. I think I will stay here all through the winter; in fact, I have an idea that I may buy a house here."

He had completely misunderstood my reply, taking what I had intended as a spiritual evaluation of the place as if I had been talking about my stomach. I did not try to continue in that vein.

Luigi had been following the conversation without much interest, but at this point he said. "I find it very difficult to write anywhere. Italy's condition now is so depressing, that sometimes it all seems useless."

"Nonsense," M— said, "I get new ideas every

day. I never write less than five or ten pages a day. It's all a matter of hard work."

Luigi, too, was silenced. Jane had got up from the table with a new bottle of wine and was pouring it into everybody's glass. I was already drunk; I gulped down the new glassful because I felt hot. She filled the glass again and went on. I felt then the beginning of a headache and I wished we would get up from the table and move somewhere. I was uncomfortable and couldn't follow any of the conversation, which flowed along in little bursts and spurts. Henry sang part of a song. Cesare put an entire tomato in his mouth and tried to swallow it without chewing. Finally they began getting up.

But we didn't move very far. Only back to the beach. I really would have preferred to be indoors somewhere, but I felt completely helpless, in the power of the others, so I went along with them, first changing back into my bathing-suit. I put myself in the sun and covered my face with the towel, thinking that perhaps in this way, I could exorcise the headache, which had arrived by this time and was tremendous.

But there was no escaping the headache. And, in the same way, I felt there was no escaping the others, the group. Briefly I thought I would like to get away on my own, perhaps do some sightseeing—I remem-

69

bered my dinner with two old ladies in New York, friends of my family. They loved Capri. "You must be sure to see the Blue Grotto," one of them had said. "And the villa of Axel-Munthe," the other went on. "You must be sure, Bill, to see both of those things before you come back to America." For a moment it occurred to me that I should see these things, that it would be fun to get on a bus and go to Anacapri with a group of tourists and be shown about Axel-Munthe's villa by a respectful, completely informed guide, who would answer everyone's questions, and perhaps afterward I would feel that I had *done* something during my hours in Capri, that I had seen something worthwhile and thereby acquired something to take home with me, something with an established value, like a piece of money.

This impulse lasted only a moment, however. The sun was hot and made me feel heavy and weak. The others went in and out of the water. Henry got another bottle of wine, but drank most of it himself because nobody else wanted any. I said, "I have a headache" to Luigi, but he simply said "That's too bad" and rolled over in the sand, not taking me seriously.

Gradually, though, the headache became the chief reality of the afternoon for me. Later when we all went up to the square in a taxi, there was much crowding. I had to sit on Jane's lap, while Cesare sat on the hood of the car, and rolled back and forth, pretending he was going to fall off. Jane screamed, squeezing me, her arms across my chest, and laughing, too. Henry shouted a bet to Cesare that he wouldn't sit for a full minute without holding on. Cesare did it, then remembered that they hadn't bet anything, so he didn't know what he had won. I saw all this and felt all this, but it was removed from me by the dull throbbing in my head—all these other things were in the background.

In the square all the tables were jammed. We worked our way through them, single file, until at last we found a table vacant. Chairs had to be lifted over the heads of others. In the confusion several drinks were spilled, but nobody bothered. We ordered tea, and sat looking about.

M— was at one of the tables with his wife and another woman. Several people were pointed out to me, an actor, a painter. Finally someone said, "There's Norman Douglas." And I saw a very old, thin, fragile man walking out of the square with another man and woman. He was talking. Naturally I could not hear him, but from the way he bent his head slowly and from an occasional brief gesture, I imagined his famous conversation, elaborate and allusive, going on and

71

on as they walked down the slanting, scented street.

"Time to be drinking," Jane announced suddenly, as if a bell had just struck.

"Right" said Henry.

Cesare and O'Leary promptly started calling the waiter. Cesare made huge imperious gestures, imitating for my benefit the American tourist, pounding the table, looking around superciliously, rolling his eyes at Jane. When the waiter came at last, O'Leary paid while we were pushing our chairs back and extracting ourselves from the tangle of furniture.

It had grown dark and the other tables were mostly bare. As we left the square I noticed one couple sitting at a table in the corner. The woman was crying, sobbing noisily, making no attempt to conceal the tremendous tears that were pouring down her rather plain face. The man with her sat as if nothing were happening, looking idly off into space. The waiters either pretended not to notice or else really didn't notice. I wondered what on earth was making the woman cry so, but there was no telling.

The first bar was only partly full. I judged that a lot of people were eating their dinner and it was too early for the drinking-places to fill up. It was about seven or seven-thirty. We had a Martini around and went on to the next place.

72

Cesare and O'Leary got drunk quickly and became exuberant, making extravagant jokes of courtesy, bowing before each other as they went through doors, toasting each other in jumbled speeches. Gradually we all became drunk. Henry began speaking Italian. Luigi became more like Cesare, full of spirits, amused by his brother's jokes. Jane wanted to sing. We left one bar with her perched on the shoulders of Cesare and O'Leary, singing *j'ai deux amours*... I was drunk, but my headache only got worse. All I could think of in my drunkeness was how terribly I was suffering, how bravely I was keeping the knowledge from the others, and how unfeelingly they were enjoying themselves when I felt so awful.

The bar of the hotel where Henry and Jane were staying was too crowded. The stares of the people at the bar, properly dressed and a little stiff for Capri, dampened the spirits even of Cesare. We decided to take our drinks into the game room, which was off the bar.

It was a large room, with one window, a huge center light hanging low over a ping-pong table. As soon as we were in the room, the flow of good humor which had been cut off temporarily in the bar started again with double force. Henry started playing ping-pong with Jane while Cesare and O'Leary pretended to be judges. Every now and then they would interrupt the game and hold long discussions about imaginary rules. Several times they caught the ball as it flew across the table, and shouted "Take it over." Finally Henry and Jane gave up.

O'Leary and Cesare grabbed the paddles and ball and began playing. First they simply slammed the ball back and forth in imitation of a game. Then they started hitting the ball deliberately as hard as they could, as if it were a baseball. Until finally it broke. Then they slammed the pieces at each other. Jane took an ice-cube out of her glass and hit it with a paddle toward Henry, who threw it back at her glass, like a basketball, but missed. It skidded across the floor. Everyone was shouting. From time to time a waiter would come in to see what was going on and would be sent out to get drinks.

At last I couldn't stand it any longer. I had been thinking that at some point it would stop. We would go on to another hotel or bar, we would eat, someone would pass out. But none of these things happened.

"I'm going on to bed," I said to Luigi in one of the moments of comparative silence.

He seemed surprised. "Why? It's so early. We haven't even eaten dinner. It's only about nine-thirty or ten."

"I'm tired and my head aches," I said crossly.

I got up with the intention of leaving, then remembered that I didn't know where we were staying. Luigi had arranged about a room that morning while I had stayed with Cesare in the square. I was annoyed that Luigi had to leave the others and accompany me back to our room.

"Good-night," Jane called above the shouts of the others, who had started playing catch with their glasses and were throwing them faster and faster so that the supposed catcher would miss them and they would break.

I didn't answer her, but walked out of the room and followed Luigi down the steps and into the street. The night was warm and light; the air seemed thin.

Luigi had engaged a room in a sort of tenement. I had told him that I didn't want to spend money on Capri and he had agreed that we should be economical. When I saw the ugly iron beds and the jug and bowl for washing and the hideous wallpaper, I wished that I had saved my thriftiness for another time and had gone to a hotel. But it was too late and I was too tired. I threw my bathing suit and towel on a chair, took off my shoes, socks, pants, and shirt and got in the uncomfortable bed. I had brought no pyjamas or toothbrush with me.

"Is there anything I can do for you?" Luigi said, rather apologetic now, since I had made it so petulantly evident that I was annoyed.

"You might get me some water," I said in a dying voice. "I'm thirsty."

"I think there's some in this carafe." He took it from the bureau and put it on the rickety table between the beds. "If there's nothing else, I guess I'll hunt up the others. They'll probably be about ready to eat."

"Good-night, then," I said.

"Good-night. I'll probably be in early. I'll try not to wake you up."

"Oh, that's all right," I said, quite sure that I wouldn't be able to sleep a wink.

He left, and I shut my eyes. Then all the night sounds of Capri assailed my ears. Our room had a long French window that opened on a tiny balcony over one of the main streets of the town. From below I could hear the shuffling of rope-soled shoes coming up from the street, the fragments of passing conversations. Someone whistled. In the distance I could hear a song, perhaps from a radio.

The idea of going to sleep without having looked out of the window, without having seen the view, orienting myself, seemed impossible. I forced myself out of bed and stood for a while, in my shorts, on the dark little balcony. The street beneath slanted sharply up to the right, the direction of the square. Most of the windows were dark, but farther up, on the hill above the town, there were lights, made so small by the distance that they could be mistaken for stars. There was a muted sound of jazz, accented by weak thumps, that came from a night-club near the square. In one of the rooms across the street a girl was singing, much too loud for that time of night when children would be asleep and the houses quiet, but her voice, not trained or lovely but true, flooded out of one of the dark windows and filled the street.

Satisfied with what I had seen, I stumbled back to the bed. My headache seemed better, and in a few minutes I was asleep.

Naturally Luigi and I both woke early the next morning. The sun came pouring through the French window and the noises in the street began very early. Neither of us felt well after our unaccustomed drinking of the night before, but at least I didn't have that headache any longer—only a general malaise and shakiness, which I recognized. Added to this, there was a sense of having behaved stupidly to Luigi; I felt really apologetic and as a result was especially friendly and considerate. But Luigi had apparently forgotten all about it, or had never thought about it particularly, because he gave no sign that he thought I should make up for anything, nor did he ask about my headache. We simply talked over our common symptoms.

We went out at last to the barber and had ourselves shaved. This always improves my disposition and afterwards I felt just like having my morning coffee.

We sat at one of the tables in the square. I was glad it was too early for the others, because I wanted to find out something more about them from Luigi. He had talked to Cesare about them the night before.

"Who is this O'Leary?" I asked him.

Ollieri, he told me, was from Milan. Until a few years ago he had been poor, although of a good family, and had lived the life of a playboy without means, borrowing, gambling, finally marrying a wife who had a little money for a dowry. Ollieri took this money just as the war ended and went off to Switzerland with it on a vacation. There he happened to meet an American general, who wanted to learn how to ski and asked Ollieri to teach him. During the weeks that they spent skiing together, the general took quite a shine to Ollieri and promised to do something for him.

"And…?" I was getting a little impatient since Luigi was digressing at length on the *simpatia* that the two felt for each other.

"Well, later on the general was leaving Italy and

had to dispose of twelve Army camps, their material and so on. So he *gave* them to Ollieri."

"He *what?*"

"Gave them. He wasn't very smart, that general, I don't suppose. Because of course, the Italian government took them over, but Ollieri made a protest and showed papers the general had given him, so the Italian government gave him a lot of money—a million or so—and he bought a steel mill. Then he set his brother to running the steel mill, left his wife in Milan, and came down here."

"The whole story seems incredible to me," I said. "Do you believe it yourself?"

"I know it sounds funny, but stranger things than that happened in Italy in these years. Cesare swears that it's the truth and says that everybody on Capri knows all about it."

"I imagine that everybody on Capri knows all about everything that happens to anyone else around."

"Pretty much," Luigi agreed. "What did you think of Jane, by the way?"

"She's all right." I was non-committal, because I thought that Luigi had found her rather attractive. To me she seemed the usual blonde chorus-girl, slightly veneered with culture, well-groomed, but otherwise the classic gold-digger.

"She's really interesting. She's here with Henry, you know—he's a film producer in London and has lots of money. But she does whatever she wants. She's very clever, making him pay for everything for her, and then she goes to bed with the people she wants to. She's slept with Ollieri a lot, and Cesare says he has had her, too, but he may just be boasting."

"I'm afraid I don't see anything particularly clever about her. To me she's a rather usual phenomenon and not very attractive either. I'm sure Cesare isn't bragging when he says he's slept with her. I should think he could do much better than that around here."

"I like her. She's amusing, you know." Luigi was bound to defend her. I realized that for him—as for Cesare—she was the more exotic for being English. Just as in America one likes to brag of love affairs with French girls or Italian girls, just because they are foreign.

I didn't feel like pursuing the subject, so I agreed that she was probably very amusing. At that point Cesare appeared, waving and smiling. He came up and dropped into a chair.

"Well, how are your heads this morning? I hope that little example of our home-like evenings on Capri didn't upset you both. Of course, Bill left much too early. What happened to you anyway? You crept away quietly, saying nothing. I thought you were with us for a long time after you had left, and Jane didn't discover you had gone until she was saying goodnight to everyone. Really, you might have told us where you were off to—not that we would have interfered with any plans of yours for anything in the world. We understand things here." He smiled and ordered a chocolate, as if I weren't expected to answer.

"I went to bed," I said lamely. "I was feeling tired."

"We will enquire no further," Cesare said, turning to Luigi. "And you, worthy older brother?"

"Don't get too affectionate," Luigi said jokingly. "I have to produce you at home no later than this afternoon."

"Ah, yes. To be sure. Well, let's be in no hurry. There is a boat at five, I believe."

"There's also one at twelve-thirty. We will take that one. Do you have any packing to do? You ought to be doing it."

Cesare shrugged. "I don't think I'll bother to take anything. I'm just going home and coming right back."

"You'd better pack something. I don't relish the idea of your borrowing from me all the time in case your stay is extended. I'll just come and help you …right now."

"Oh, all right," Cesare submitted, taking it all as a joke.

I told them I would stay there in the square and wait for them. I bought some postal cards and sent them off to my family and a few friends. As I was writing them, I noticed M— going by and I smiled and nodded at him.

For a moment he didn't recognize me, then smiled—doubly friendly to make up—and came over.

"Still here? I thought Capri didn't agree with you." He spoke very brusquely as if he were accusing me and wanted me to defend myself.

"I didn't mean exactly that." I felt a little off guard. "I meant that I would have difficulty doing anything worthwhile here. Capri doesn't seem to a me a very creative place. Most of the people…"

"The *people*. You mean these monsters that come here in the good weather. They aren't the people of Capri. You should be here in the winter, when there are none of these types around. Then you would see what the place is like. Don't be mistaken about Capri. It's a real town underneath, like any other place. There's a great deal of misery here. The inhabitants gouge as much money as they can out of the tourists during the good months because it has to last them all during the rest of the year. And it never does. They end up hungry and underfed like people in every other part of Italy. You should see the town in the cold months when the hotels are empty and the expensive restaurants are all closed. It's a fine place. During the tourist season, you just have to ignore the others, the invaders. Come back, though, in a few months and see for yourself."

"I'd like to."

"Excuse me, if I rush off. Here come some of the people I told you to ignore. I have to practice what I've preached."

He shook hands and went off—in time to miss Henry and Jane, who appeared at the entrance to the square. They saw me and came over. After greeting one another casually, we began desultory conversation about our drinking, our hangovers, the number of bars we had visited. Jane described several incidents that had occurred after my leaving. Henry, who has been in New York a number of times, began to discuss bars there, describing each familiarly. Most of them I haven't seen, so his conversation meant very little to me.

Finally they got up. "You coming down to the beach?" Jane asked.

"No, I'm going to stay up here for a while." I didn't tell them that we were leaving. It would have been so pointless to have to exchange goodbyes with them—they cared nothing about me nor I about them. By now they will have forgotten me entirely.

"Well, see you later."

"Have a nice swim," I said, watching them hail a taxi and start the trip down.

The entrances and exits into the square were taking on the strange, coincidental quality of a play. No sooner were they gone than Luigi and Cesare came hack, the latter carrying a small bag and dressed in a regular suit—still with his pink shirt, though.

"The others just went down to the beach," I said.

"Oh, I'm sorry I missed them. I should have explained that I was going." Cesare looked back at the taxi-stand as if they might still be there.

"Never mind." Luigi, I thought, was a little relieved that they had gone. I was too. Cesare's docility might have been weakened if they had pictured any amusing project for the morning.

We were prepared to sit at that table in the square until time for the boat. I had thought it might be dull, but actually a series of Cesare's friends (which seemed to include the entire population of the island—temporary and permanent) drifted by and stopped to chat: the porter from Jane and Henry's hotel, an old English lady who spoke to C. in abominable Italian and thereby amused him, several girls. Finally a boy about Cesare's age came through the square carrying a fishing pole and a creel. When he saw us he gave a shout of recognition and came over.

"Oo-ee, Cesare!" He was obviously Neapolitan. Well-bred and good-looking, taller than many Neapolitans, dark, curly hair.

Luigi explained to me that this boy, Andrea, was another like Cesare, who came from a good family in the city but had no money and didn't want to work so he lived at Capri, fishing at times, scrounging meals from people who liked his looks and conversation.

We talked for a few minutes, then Andrea got up. "Excuse me for rushing off, but I have to go and change my clothes. I'm going out to dinner." He said this with the air of someone who announces he is going to marry a movie star or an English princess.

"Well," said Cesare, accenting his words carefully and skeptically, "if it's *true,* good appetite."

The bell of the church began striking noon. "Shouldn't we go down and get on the boat?" I said, impatient to be off.

"It's a little early," Luigi said, "but I suppose we might as well."

The funicular seemed to rush down the hill. I stood in the front compartment, at the operator's elbow, and watched the port and the little boat hurry toward us. When we stood finally on the deck, I looked up and saw it all above me: the delicately tinted villas, the rocky hill, the ruined Saracen tower. And as the boat, at last, moved out from the shore, I felt relieved, as if I had escaped from something. Cesare and Luigi settled down on the wooden benches and slept, while I stood at the rail to watch the familiar shore drift by: Massa, Sorrento, Castelammare ...all of them in a shower of sunlight, El Doradoes.

Signora Fabbri welcomed us back with a huge dinner, fussing over Cesare as if he had just got back from winning a war, no thought of reproving him or sulking. Cesare takes all of her attentions with non-chalance, as if he deserved them and more. I think Signor Fabbri is amused by this a little, but the quiet melancholy of his face is not dissipated by Cesare's extravagant clowning. After dinner when Luigi and I lay down to rest, Cesare and his father went off to the office presumably for the dressing-down for which Cesare was brought back.

Later in the afternoon Cesare came back while Luigi and I were still on our beds. He opened the shutters to light the room up and began rummaging his bureau drawer.

"What did father say to you?" Luigi asked him. I, too, was eager to know.

"Nothing important. I haven't time to discuss it with you now. I have to go out." He was tearing off his pink shirt and putting on a clean white one. He also changed his shoes, then went out.

Luigi and I went to a movie, then came home. Cesare did not come in for supper. In fact, we have no idea when he did come in, because it was after all of us were asleep.

This morning he was up early and out before we were. His mother asked him where he was going, but he just whistled and looked important and winked at Luigi and me. Later Luigi went to the club to play tennis and I am taking advantage of the solitude—a thing not easily achieved in this household—to write down these notes on the past two days.

Saturday.

Big scene this morning between Cesare and his mother. She came into the room where the three of us are sleeping (I have C.'s bed, so he sleeps on a cot—in spite of my offers to do so) and began shouting at Cesare, who was just barely awake. At first I didn't understand what it was all about, and the signora was not exactly coherent. Cesare just laughed, and Luigi kept saying, "Is it completely impossible to sleep until a decent hour in this house?"

Signora Fabbri ignored him completely and went on verbally belaboring Cesare, who became more and more amused as he gradually woke up. I finally began to understand the situation. Apparently Cesare had sold his other pair of shoes—the good ones—for two thousand lire, then had gone to the club and gambled until he had won about twenty thousand, then he had bet that and lost it, so had ended up with nothing.

The curious thing about Signora Fabbri's argument was that she didn't seem to be angry with Cesare for gambling or for selling his shoes but rather for not quitting when he was a winner. She would turn to me for support, explaining all the things Cesare could have done with the twenty thousand: bought back his shoes, paid some of his debts, bought himself a nice coat. "Non è giusto, Bill?"

I nodded, of course, agreeing with her out of a sense of duty, although the precise moral values of the situation were not quite clear to me. Every time I would nod, Cesare winked and smiled at me, as if it were a joke that his mother was so mad and asked me to be on her side. The more he would smile, the madder she got, naturally, so the scene wore on. She stood at the door of the bathroom and shouted at Cesare while he was shaving. And finally she accompanied him to the door, still arguing, until at the last minute, she calmed herself long enough to say, "Now don't be late for dinner, and if you are in town, stop by your grandmother's and pick up that copy of Harper's Bazaar I lent her. Luigi promised to get it for me yesterday and forgot." Cesare exited and the house was quiet.

Sunday.

Cesare has gone. Last night he borrowed a thousand lire at the club and played chemin de fer all evening, ending up winner with about twenty-five thousand. This morning he got up very early—and took the boat out to Capri. The signora came into our room while Luigi and I were having our coffee in bed. Laughing she told us all about it. "What do you think of that, Bill? Twenty-five thousand." It seemed to her a huge joke that he should have won more last night than he had lost the night before. "I do hope he'll buy some shoes with some of it."

The house seems much deader now that he has gone. Already I am missing his clowning and his blasphemous remarks intended to scandalize his mother. Luigi seems to think that nothing else could have been expected of Cesare; there is no talk of going out to get him another time. Apparently Signor Fabbri has reproved him and that is considered that.

Monday.

Postal cards. Mother said to me before I left, "You must certainly send a line to X., even a card, it would be such a nice thing to do." Since my arrival here I have written so few letters, beyond a weekly despatch to the family, that I am occasionally visited by the idea that when I finally return home I will be completely out of touch with everyone, will have no friends. So yesterday afternoon, at last, I bought a handful of views of the city when I went by the tobacconist's, and this morning I took them with me to the Middleton Tearoom, where I sat writing them and drinking a noontime vermouth.

It was fun writing them, selecting the proper card, addressing it, filling in the left-hand blank space with two appropriate remarks. I like to think then that the card would arrive and give—as mother said —pleasure, causing the person to think briefly of me in a foreign country, to wonder about me there, perhaps to write to me. But at the same time, I couldn't help thinking of the inadequacy of even the best letters. Even if, in writing the letters, I wrote exactly the thoughts that went through my mind, and if the person I wrote to replied in the same fashion, it would be inaccurate, false. In an honest conversation, one says what he thinks, but in listening to the other person, he modifies what he has said, or exaggerates it; his position changes, his emotions toward his hearer vary.

All of this occurred to me as I scrawled on the cards, making no attempt to say anything important, only a greeting and a commonplace.

First I sent a card to Mrs. Hogben, an old friend of the family's who had seen me a short while before I left. "Do write me," she had said. "I would so like to know how dear old Naples has changed, if it has been very badly damaged. I often wonder if the Brittanique is still standing—how sweet a place it was—and Caflisch, the most wonderful pastry place on the Toledo. Please, please, Bill send me a card and tell me all about the city...."

A view of the Via Partenope for Mrs. Hogben. *Had a nice trip over. Caflisch and the Brittanique still going strong. My best to Mr. H. and the girls.* Perhaps, though, I should have written differently. Perhaps I should have said: If you came here now, Mrs. Hogben, you would find your hotel, your pastry shop, your obliging guide—all the same as before, you would be perfectly content. Probably when you saw the destroyed areas around the dock (you would pass them on your way to Pompeii), you would say how much Italy has changed, and you would tell your friends at

91

home that the country hasn't yet recovered from the war. And yet, for you, this change would be so slight it would be negligible, mere conversation fodder. But maybe that is your chief reason for coming here? To see things that you can talk about at home, buy inlaid tables for outrageous prices in Sorrento, leather telephone-book covers in Florence, a tortoise-shell vanity set. Really you move only in yourself, your external environment has so little effect on you, why do you come here at all?...

For Mother a picture of the Palazzo. *This is the place I am staying. Our apartment marked. All well here. Love...* And yet I know how inadequate this picture will be for you. You will want to know at once about the bathrooms and the food and if I have enough blankets. I am warm enough, yes, and the food and the bathroom are good, though at home they are no doubt better. But even if I wrote you all this, it wouldn't satisfy you, but would lead only once more to that basic question which you have been wanting to ask me all along; why? Why are you there? And I thank you for never having asked me, because I wouldn't know how to answer it properly. It is a question I have asked myself, but the only possible reply is vague and unsatisfying: I came because I wanted to find something I couldn't find anywhere else, an attitude toward life, a way of thinking and feeling… Everyone has to find this for himself and where he can. To me, Italy seemed the right place… But would you have understood this if I had told you? Probably you would. Probably you understood anyway…

Vance. I would have liked to get you a view of the Hospital where we both worked on that hill we swore at a thousand times, but the best I could do was a cockeyed photo of the Gallery. *Thought you might recognize this. Lots of changes. How about a letter? Love to Tina.* But are you really interested in all this? Will this photograph have any significance for you, or will it only recall some sad-happy moments, now without any force? I felt when I saw you last, in the midst of the crowd at that farewell party, that you were not entirely in sympathy with my going. I thought that perhaps you had the idea I was wrong, that I should do as you have done, marry and settle down, start a career, grow up. But this trip was never intended as a flight into the past, and it hasn't been. I hope when I come back that you will see this, see in me that I have grown through coming back here.

For N. there is no card particularly appropriate. A general panorama of the city. *Thanks for your letters, darling. Will write when I get settled a bit. Miss you very much. All my love.* It's true that I miss you, especially when I had your long, interesting letter, full of news of our friends, of New York, of the things we share an interest in. But already I am wondering what to write you. Sometimes in New York, I would suddenly feel far away from you, sometimes when we had finished making love and I held you in my arms, I felt as if I were holding a corpse. But now I feel even more remote, as if none of my long, leisurely days would interest you. Surely it can make no difference to you that last night I went to the Supercinema and saw Loretta Young and Joseph Cotten in a bad film whose name I have already forgotten. Also, I must admit to myself that the list of things you have seen, the new plays, the art shows, seem without importance except that you were there. And I am beginning to be afraid that when I come back we will talk, each of us, a foreign language. What will we say? I will have gone on in one direction and you, I think, in a different one. What a risk it was, leaving. And yet I knew that. Was I right? Should I have stayed and been with you instead of gambling you against this? Only you make me question the rightness of my coming....

It was nearly two when I had finished these four cards. Not much to show for a morning's work—a few sentences written. But I dawdled so over each. I put all the unwritten ones in my pocket (tomorrow I must make a list of people and send each a card. I can write nearly the same thing to them all), and the others I mailed on my way home to dinner.

Friday.

A great day. This morning there was the ceremonial visit of Signora Fabbri's mother, Luigi's grandmother. Preceded by a telephone call which set Rosaria off (she rushed around talking to herself about "la nonna"), the old lady finally arrived about eleven.

I was in my room, reading. Luigi was writing at the table. We had left the door open and from the adjoining living-room we got all the sound effects of the arrival. Signora Fabbri herself went to the door; no sooner had she opened it than we began to hear the voice of her mother, obviously in a highly nervous state.

They went at once into the signora's room, but even so we could hear the steady flow of the old lady's complaint. And occasionally certain words, exclamations, were quite clear. *Figlia,* the grandmother would moan, *Figlia mia.*

"What in the world is wrong?" Tact battled with my curiosity and lost quickly. I had to ask Luigi for an explanation.

95

"Oh, my grandmother is upset about Rina, I suppose. That's her standard complaint." He showed no interest at all in the moans that were coming from the other room; he didn't even look up from his writing.

"Does your grandmother know about Rina and her son?" I imagined the old lady's concern about the immoral liaison.

"Naturally," Luigi answered. "Everybody in Naples knows about it. But the old lady doesn't mind that; it's just that every now and then Rina does something that gets on her nerves, then she comes over here to complain to mother about it. Anyhow we'll know all about it at lunch; my grandmother believes in the repetition of everything."

I went on trying to read, but with no success. Finally the signora came to call me to the table. She smiled at me broadly, as if including me in a private joke.

The conversation at the table was not really conversation but a monologue by the nonna, interrupted by soothing purrs on the part of the signora, and ridiculing remarks from Luigi, to whom the old lady paid no attention at all.

I had difficulty following the recital, and Luigi was delighted to translate it to me in English. Apparently the original cause of this outburst was Rina's criticism of the cooking at the nonna's house. This remark of Rina's had led to a violent argument, in the course of which another son in the family, Bruno's brother, had announced that he was a communist and, being a communist, approved of free love: hence Rina and Bruno were doing the right thing. That was the final blow, apparently.

Today nonna went through the scene, word by word, repeating every so often her favorite phrase about Rina: *pazza da legare,* which Luigi translates "mad to be tied up".

I felt a little embarrassed through it all and tried not to laugh, the more ridiculous it got. With all her weeping and excitement, the old lady has a great dignity and style. Afterwards Luigi told me that she was, in her youth, very beautiful and a talented amateur singer. She was among the "black" aristocracy in Rome and, according to Luigi, she insists that she could have been, if she had wanted, the mistress of the Pope. There was nothing definite, but she is sure that he looked at her several times in a certain way.

Tuesday.

If I write a novel about Naples, it will have to take place at this time of year. I would like to distill this weather into a paragraph or two—impossible job. Like so much about the city, the weather is incredible. These mornings when I go out, having had only a tiny cup of coffee, I feel drunk in the light balmy air. The sky, even blue, is spread out like a sheet of wallpaper. And as I pass along the outside of the park, following Via Caracciolo, the sea glistens along the shore, hissing like an animal. Anything could happen in weather like this. And yet, oddly enough, I am quite conscious that it is autumn, in spite of the warmth and the leafy trees and the people swimming; the most exciting characteristic of this weather is a certain moribund quality in it. At times this disturbs me.

Saturday.

I have been here three weeks today. The days dissolve one into the next and I am unconscious of time passing. Only a few events stand out, a few new people. Already I feel myself habituated; I pass a day, two days, without speaking a word of English and do not feel the lack. Little things: riding the busses, using the telephone—are no longer adventures. I do not feel a foreigner.

All this means that the days have had their effect on me, but the process has been imperceptible. And has it been valuable? Is this what I came for? To be able to order a meal or find my way about downtown.

The last few days I have been attacked by a kind of uneasiness, as if I were not doing something that I should be doing. Naples has made me feel that traveling is a passive occupation; the voyager allows himself to be acted upon, and, as a result, he is broadened, improved. Now I am reacting. No, I say to myself, the traveler should be creative, should *do*.

What? I cannot decide. Go through the museum with his guidebook? Buy all the postal cards of famous spots? Ask questions of the natives and memorize the birth-rate and death-rate?

Luigi is no help at all. I do not even bother to discuss this with him, because he would accuse me of being American and of having to moralize about everything. He is right. But I think I am right, too; or at least, I am this way. And I must keep looking for the reply to my own question.

Wednesday.

As I was lying in bed this morning, I began to think how long I have been in Naples and how little I have done. I tried to make some mental tally of Things Achieved: one or two books read, Capri seen (?), and that was all. Not very impressive. Inspired, or

99

rather, egged on by this record of inactivity, I decided that I would do some sightseeing, at least *one* thing a day, until I felt I know Naples. It is ridiculous for me to have stayed here this long and not have seen anything, not even the Museum.

So I chose the museum for today. As we were having our coffee, I asked Luigi what tram one took to go to the museum.

"I don't know. You'll have to ask Rosaria. What are you going up that way for?" This is a long speech for him in the morning; he takes hours usually to wake up.

"I thought I'd go to the museum this morning."

The announcement seemed to wake him up. He rolled over and faced me. "So the tourist in you is coming out at last?" He laughed.

"No," I protested, "it's just that I thought…"

"No excuses." To him the joke got funnier and funnier.

When his mother came in then, he told her about it. "Of course, Bill is right," she said, but I could see she was amused at Luigi's teasing me.

Finally Rosaria came in with the coffee, I found out about the tram, and the subject was dropped. But Luigi's amusement was evident later, when I got up promptly, washed, and dressed—at nine-thirty, long before our usual hour for protracted rising and dressing.

"I'll be back for dinner," I said as I left, smiling at Luigi and the Signora, amused by their amusement.

This morning the weather was unpleasant, cloudy and colder. I felt a hostility in it, as I rode in the bus into the center of town. And the tram I took there was crowded, and for some reason, I wasn't amused by the jostling and the talk.

I got off in front of the museum and looked at it. The building is certainly oppressive from the outside. Certain windows are boarded up; it is decaying and looks abandoned. In fact, I asked a passer-by if it were open, before I went up the steps to the door.

It *was* open, but the high, dark vestibule looked empty at first glance. Then I discerned an attendant in the gloom.

"How much?" I asked him.

But he referred me to a little table at the other end of the room, where I bought a ticket. This I took back to the first man, who tore off a corner and opened a wicket for me to pass into the main rooms of the museum.

It is a strange and upsetting place, like a warehouse or morgue. The rooms are huge and overpowering. In the main hall I was, I must admit, depressed by some colossal heads of Vespasian—fully fifty times life size. The ugliness and vulgarity of that obese face seemed to look down on me from all sides. In another room I found shelves full of recovered bits of statues; arms, legs, ears. In the darkness it seemed some kind of chamber of horrors, or perhaps a place where a bomb had just fallen and blown everyone to bits. Inevitably I was reminded of the war.

The one light touch was another room, somewhat brighter than the others, where the famous Herculaneum dancers are exposed. The series of six or so draped female figures in their rigid, yet dancing attitudes is beautiful; but the blackness of the bronze and their eyes, which are whitened, produce a slightly ridiculous effect. I thought they looked—lined up in that way—like a minstrel show, and I half-expected one of them to come out with, "Tell me, Mr. Bones," or "Why did the chicken, etc...."

I suppose more as a reaction to my former depression than anything else, this struck me as hilarious, and I laughed. At the very moment I was laughing, some Swedish tourists, complete with funny linen caps and *Guide Bleu*, came into their room, their faces full of that museum piety that people assume the minute they have bought their ticket. This made me laugh still more, to their complete astonishment and indignation.

I thought then that I had better leave while I was still in a good humor, so I hurried past them, through the main hall, trying to avoid Vespasian, out into the street.

It was still cloudy and unpleasant, but I walked down to the foot of Via Roma, took the bus and came home. Luigi asked me how my sightseeing had been and I told him about the Swedish tourists, which delighted him.

Tomorrow the program continues. I am thinking of going to Herculaneum, inspired by the dancers, I guess; but I was there once during the war and liked it and now I'd like to go back. Later in the afternoon when I've got up, I'll go by American Express and find out about trains and busses. If only the weather is more pleasant.

Thursday.

Herculaneum. It was a perfect day for going. When I got up—earlier than usual, to Luigi's continued amusement—the sun was shining down on the sea beneath my window, smooth as a plate. I was afraid it might be hot, but afterwards, when I was walking down to Mergellina to take the tram, a breeze had sprung up and the day seemed vivified and propitious.

I had decided to go down there by the little local train from the Circumvesuviana station. I suppose I chose this method more because I like the name of the station than for any more intelligent reason. But I am just as glad. The trip down was delightful: a series of little stations, some of them still showing the effects of the war, some fertile gardens, and neatly divided countryside, looking old and cared for, like a superannuated pet. And always, from the right-hand windows of the train there was the sea, brilliant blue and deceptively warm-looking.

As I rode down in the crowded third-class compartment, I thought of my visit to Herculaneum during the war. It was only a glimpse, really, a stolen leisure moment one day when I was driving my ambulance, empty by luck, from Naples to Castellammare. The brief stay there remained in my mind chiefly because of the guides. They were all one family: a grandfather, with opulent white moustaches, his sons and grandsons. Then they welcomed me to Herculaneum as if it were their private property, as if they had created it themselves. I remember the young grandson who showed me around, saying every so often, "You won't see anything like this at Pompeii." And he would point to some relief or mosaic, bursting with family pride.

They were all there today when I arrived: the old gentleman sitting behind the ticket window, the rest of the family lounging around the gate. They sold me my ticket with great cordiality, reminding me again of the pleasant moment in the war when I had been there. I was almost tempted to say something, to tell them I had seen them all before and had remembered them for nearly four years. But I knew that it would have been ridiculous; they would have smiled and chatted politely and so on. Better to keep that past moment to myself.

I told them I didn't need a guide, and they let me go on in alone. The ruins were deserted then, and I felt as if I were the first to discover them. Seen this way, they do not appear so ancient, but more as if the disaster had occurred last week, instead of in 79 A.D. or whenever it was.

It is strange that ruins should be as attractive as these. One would think that anything so tragic and dead would be, inevitably, a little depressing. But no. Herculaneum makes me wish I could live there. Today, of course, was the ideal day for seeing it: the slight breeze from the sea (which you can watch from any point in the town, its motion contrasting with the stillness of the ruins), the clear sky, the full fragrance of the oleanders that bloom everywhere, giving the place an odor of life.

I don't know how much time I spent wandering

up and down the empty, narrow, stone-paved streets. I looked into doorways, turned up alleys and found myself retracing steps. Once I saw, cut lightly into a brick, the inscription: "Nobby Waterman, Manchester," the relic of some British soldier who had found his way here. For a moment I was filled with anger at this desecration, but then reflecting, my feeling was changed.

I'm afraid I realized that I, too, have been tempted a number of times to write my name on some ancient monument. And thinking it over, I began to understand why. I think that, being impressed by something particularly old and beautiful, one instinctively wants to associate or identify himself with it, as if to perpetuate a little of himself by sharing the permanence of the work of art. To extend, perhaps, that fine moment one has on experiencing real beauty or even (one can't say the Pyramids are beautiful and yet I felt this sensation there) tangible history.

Playing with this idea a bit, I thought it might be compared to the impulse one has to waggle his head or tap his foot in time with great music. This is something I detest in others, and yet I discover myself doing it unconsciously. I suppose I want to share in the act of creating, or re-creating, the abstract work of art. When I listen to the Ninth Symphony and jog my knee, it is as if I wanted to be a sub-Beethoven, or perhaps a sub-Koussevitsky anyway.

Eventually I was aware that it was late and I had better go. As I was walking up the flower-lined path to the entrance, I saw a sleek car with a Milan license drive up and a large family got out; I left in time, before others came to disturb "my" ruins by talking among them. I said good-bye to the old gentleman, had a beer in a cafe up the street, and took the train in time to get home for dinner.

Friday.

Last night Luigi and I were out late (the movies here don't begin until nearly ten), so that I slept late this morning and even when I woke, I was still a little tired from yesterday's full program.

I thought that today I would carry on the sightseeing plan by visiting Virgil's tomb, which is not very far away. It was nearly eleven when I finally left the house, and afraid that I would be late for lunch, I took the bus to Mergellina and walked from there. The tomb is tucked into a little patch of green between the Mergellina Station and the superstructure of the tunnel that leads out to Bagnoli.

It was closed. Through the iron bars of the gate I could see a pebbled walk and a clump of trees, and that was all. I rattled the gate a bit and looked around to see if there is a keeper, but nothing happened. Finally a passer-by explained to me that today is some sort of holiday, and the place is closed.

This information seemed to cut me adrift. Since I had no other plans for the morning and it was really too late to do anything else I went on back to the Palazzo. The Signora was out calling, and Luigi had gone off on some errand.

It was unusual for me to be at home and alone at that hour and for a little while I couldn't make up my mind to do anything, but finally I took up the book I am reading (a collection of contemporary Italian stories) and sat with it out on the terrace.

Saturday.

Today I did nothing. After my disappointment yesterday with Virgil's tomb, I didn't seem to have the energy to make any plans for today. I stayed in bed until quite late, then went with Luigi to his mother's tailor's where he had to deliver some cloth. We came home for dinner, and are now resting. Tonight there is a new movie at the Filangieri.

Monday.

I suppose to the people I met and the places I

saw in those crowded weeks in Naples in '44, I was simply one of the numerous Americans that had started filing through their lives before I arrived and continued after I left. But to me, each spot and each face became invested with individual, permanent significance. Sometimes I think I am gifted with total recall of those days, because I can remember people I met for only a moment and can almost recite from memory little, passing conversations, that everyone else will have long forgotten.

This thought occurred to me yesterday when Luigi mentioned Carlo Savello, not even thinking that I knew him. Indeed, I knew him very well and his long, cadaverous face stayed with me during my years in America, as much a part of my recollection of Naples as the line of its shore or the smell of its twisting alleys.

We saw each other only for a moment, one afternoon shortly before I sailed. Luigi and I were strolling along Via Chiaia, among the dust and rubble of that once busy thoroughfare, when we came upon Peppino, who stopped us to talk. As we were conversing, Carlo came by and I was introduced. He looked terrible: white face, eyes watering, his clothes in rags. Peppino asked him if he had had any luck (I found out later that he had just then come from applying for a job as a waiter) and he said no, but quickly changed the subject to talk of poetry. After a moment, he went on his way, after telling Peppino he wanted to show him some new things he had done.

The others talked about him for a moment and I learned the hopelessness of his poverty, his hunger, and his illness. And immediately he became a symbol for me: this boy who, in spite of all this, could talk only of poetry and made appointments with friends to discuss his latest work. He seemed another personification of that spirit I felt all around me then.

It was only natural, therefore, that I should want to see him again, when I heard his name mentioned, so casually, by Luigi. I have thought about him since my return, but I hadn't asked for news of him, mostly because I was a little afraid of what I would hear. When I saw him he seemed to have the mark of death on his forehead.

I didn't explain all this to Luigi, but simply said that I did remember meeting Carlo and that I had liked him and would be pleased to see him again. Luigi suggested that we go over there this evening; Carlo is married now and has a baby. They don't live far away.

I can't quite picture him with a family. Luigi seemed a little reluctant about going, as if he and

Carlo had rather drifted apart in these years. But his reluctance only makes me more curious. I suppose it is only Carlo's marriage that separates them a bit. Young married men here have to lead such preoccupied lives that I imagine Luigi has few married friends.

Tuesday.

Carlo shares a large apartment with two old maiden aunts of his wife. One of them opened the door for us last night and in pantomime showed Luigi and me into Carlo's study, which used to be the dining room apparently. The ancient women of the apartment are obviously responsible for its decoration and furnishings; as I sat looking around and waiting, I wondered how Carlo managed to write anything in that dark, heavy room with its brown wallpaper and fringed lampshades, the scenery of despair.

After a few minutes Carlo came in from the next room and apologized for keeping us waiting. "Good to see you, Luigi," he said, "it's been some time." Luigi explained who I was, and I said that we had once met briefly. Naturally, he didn't remember, and anyway I have changed considerably, as Luigi said.

But Carlo has changed very little. His eyes are clearer, and he is perhaps slightly less gaunt, but he keeps that aura of the ill man and his nervous enthusiasm. This manifested itself constantly, as the three of us sat talking around the table, a confusion of his books, newspapers, magazines, bits of typescript, and frayed, spilling cigarettes.

His wife, a pale blonde with an empty, not intelligent face, came in for a moment, asked Luigi how he was and me how long I had been in Naples, then excused herself and went back to the next room, where she was putting the baby to bed. The child was being difficult, and through the door she had left open we could hear the fretting of the baby and her attempts to soothe it.

"Are you working at something, Carlo?" Luigi pointed to the scattered pages.

"Just some translating. Gabriela Mistral. Do you know her work?" he asked me.

"No, I've just heard of her. I don't know Spanish."

"Neither do I. But with a dictionary I can make out what it means." He handed me the book. "But there are some words in this one…perhaps you could help."

Together the three of us puzzled out the meaning of a little lyric about a child asleep. I didn't think it was especially impressive. Carlo, who I thought rather exaggerated the beauty of the poem, explained that he was making the translations for a new magazine that someone, a boy that Luigi knew also, was starting.

"Italy needs a new magazine, you know, Luigi. Where can a writer publish these days?"

We talked on and on of these matters; after the magazine we discussed the poets I am translating, and after them Carlo asked me a number of questions about American writers, rather dutifully I thought.

In fact, I began to notice a lack of enthusiasm in all of his talk. And in my own, too. I felt as if we were playing records to each other; we seemed to agree on everything, and yet that agreement didn't generate any warmth. The only time Carlo really spoke with feeling was when Luigi, in a pause in the conversation, asked him how things were going at the radio station.

"That damned place. If my job there weren't keeping me alive, I wouldn't go back ever." His eyes lighted up, as if dislike were really absorbing him.

"What's wrong? I thought you were getting along well there."

"Oh, you know. Malicious people... impotence, sterility, that sort of thing.

"How do you mean?" Luigi was amused, I could tell, by Carlo's anger and was baiting him a little. Carlo didn't notice.

"You've heard, I suppose, about me and Maria." Carlo's voice had sunk to a rasping stage-whisper.

113

"One falls in love. It happens. And, since we live in Naples, everyone in this entire city knows all about it."

He was talking so heavily that I was sure his wife, at least, would know all about it very quickly. But I listened, fascinated at the thought of Carlo as the dallying husband. It was completely out of character.

"It's just that she came to get me one day at work and everyone saw her and began saying things about me. You know… 'Savello brings his mistress to the station. Scandal. It must be stopped. His poor wife. Can't he be discharged.' All of this complicated by the fact of Maria's intended husband, who has a cousin who is a technician there…"

"What happened then? Are you going to be fired?" Luigi was thoroughly diverted.

"No, it's all over now. Thanks to the cousin. He told the fiancé that everyone at the radio was discussing Maria, so the boy decided to take matters into his own hands."

Carlo's whisper had become louder than ever now; he was lost in the drama of his own story.

"It was simply amazing. The boy isn't quite…you understand. But I should have thought his family would have kept firearms out of his way, somehow. It was all so incredible. He must have waited hours for me outside the station that evening; he couldn't have had any idea of how late I was going to be working. And I was so tired when I did finally finish, and then to have to dodge bullets. I can tell you. One of them whistled past my ear and I heard it hit a tree. And as I ran back into the building, I heard the second shot go off."

He acted the scene out, ducking his head; his hand, the bullet, flicked by his face. In his excitement he nearly struck the lamp; I held my breath, for fear he would knock it over and bring his wife from the next room before the story ended.

"Did he get arrested? What did Maria think of all this?" Luigi asked.

"There wasn't anyone around at that hour, and the boy apparently just walked calmly home. I haven't seen Maria since, so I don't know what her feeling about the matter was."

"Why haven't you seen Maria?"

"Her family is keeping her close to the house now, since the wedding isn't far off. And it suits me just as well; I'm not anxious to be shot and killed one evening." He laughed, and Luigi joined him.

At that moment his wife came in. She had brought some sewing with her and sat quietly working, while we went on talking for a little while. Carlo was calm again, talking in a normal voice, and I was amused and a little bewildered at his sudden change of character from the passionate, ill-starred lover to the practical man who doesn't want to be shot. None of this fitted in with my memory-idealization of him.

Soon we go up to leave. Carlo's wife came with us to the door and asked us to come back; she shook hands with me smiling, and I thought for a moment that she knew about the whole thing and just didn't care. And for a moment, thinking that she *should* care, that it was her *duty* to care, I thought she was guiltier than Carlo himself.

I said afterwards to Luigi that I didn't see quite how Carlo could manage a mistress, since he was anything but handsome or physically pre-possessing.

"You should see Maria," Luigi answered. "In the opinion of many, she is the ugliest girl in Naples. I am one of the many."

"And her fiancé? How did she manage to get him?"

"In the first place, her family is rich. And in the second place, he is a cretin and ugly, too."

Luigi was in high good humor, and I could tell that the whole situation seemed to him the height of the ridiculous: the stupid and ugly people, the gun-shots. For a little while, this annoyed me, but then I

116

realized that the ugliness of the people wasn't the real source of Luigi's entertainment; it was their seriousness that he found so absurd. I didn't tell him all I had thought and felt about Carlo; Luigi finds enough enjoyment as it is in my ideas.

Entry.

Does the question of stagnance or stasis in people, in Luigi and his family, occupy me so much only because I am young? After all, when I look forward to my own middle years, what do I imagine? Myself settled, surrounded by love and by treasured objects and happily at rest. Doesn't this amount to the same thing?

Sunday.

Tea today with Mrs. Reed, an elderly American lady, long-time resident of Naples, who had apparently got my name and address from the consulate. At one point my hostess asked me how I liked the city, etc., and we began discussing the special Neapolitan spirit.

"I have no difficulty at all in getting on with the Neapolitans, you know." She said, with the secret air of knowing a special formula.

"Really?" I asked politely.

"It's so simple. You see I'm from the South...,"

Her lush accent had already told me that, "…and I just treat the Neapolitans like the Niggras. They're very much the same: happy and childish and irresponsible."

This from a woman who has spent over ten years in Naples.

Thursday.

There is a touring company of actors playing in Naples now, and for the past couple days I have been urging Luigi to go with me one night. He was understandably reluctant, since the three plays they are giving are all supposed to be dreadful; but I finally managed to persuade him, and we went last night.

"We" means Luigi, myself, and Rina—who really did more persuading than I did. She stopped by yesterday morning, and when I mentioned something about the theater, she seized on the plan with great enthusiasm, decided exactly how we should arrange about meeting, what sort of seats we should buy, and what we should wear.

I thought we might do well to buy the seats in advance, but Luigi assured me that nobody would be there. As it turned out, the place was more crowded than either of us expected; the theater, which is rather small, was about three-quarters full. A friendly, pleasant atmosphere prevailed: people waved back and forth across the orchestra, milled around in the aisles, shaking hands and chatting as if in their club. Many of the audience stood up in their places, their backs to the stage, watching the later arrivals coming in the two entrances.

Rina stood like this, between Luigi and me, who were seated. She commented freely on all the women as they came in, criticizing their clothes, or giving us little details of their lives. Of one girl she asked us if we had heard about the duel that had been fought the week before, then she described all the story in a rather loud voice, so that I was convinced that the girl, who was sitting only a few rows ahead of us, would be sure to hear. (It seems that a former lover of hers had taken to saying *whore* in an insulting way every time he passed her on the street, and the week before a man was with her, resented this, and provoked a duel. Nobody won.)

Nearly half an hour late, the play finally began. It was a terrible late nineteenth-century thing, apparently a great favorite of the old school: it had been one of Duse's great successes. Luigi and Rina snickered all through it, nudging each other at the especially ridiculous climaxes and at the frequent awkward moments of the ingenue.

119

I was kept busy, ignoring them, trying to follow the line of the unfamiliar and rather complicated story: all about a boy who disliked his father, until he suddenly discovered that he wasn't his father, but that an old friend of the family, whom the boy *adored*, was his father really. The boy, before all this, had been wanting to go off on an exploring expedition to get away from his unhappy home life, and his doting mother had been trying to prevent the plan, but she finally gives the young man her consent, when it turns out that his father, her ex-lover, was going to go along.

All this was so completely absurd, that I had difficulty believing that people really were taking it seriously, but Luigi, when I told him this during the first interval, said: "Just look around you in the audience. Except for a few young people who have come out of snobbism, the rest of the audience are all people in middle age, who remember seeing the great Eleanora in this when they were young, and they're back now suffering through every moment all over again, and enjoying themselves to the full. Middle class Italian taste in many ways has never got beyond D'Annunzio—early D'Annunzio."

Certainly the spectators were responsive. There were numerous curtain calls at the end of each act; and when we left at the end of the play, the thunderous, enthusiastic applause of the audience was still ringing in our ears, when we were well out of the theater and into the street.

Inevitably we discussed the play a bit. Luigi jokingly laid the blame of it all on me and swore he would never go anywhere again at my suggestion. Rina had to admit she had enjoyed herself and, in mock protection, put her hand through my arm and drew me away from Luigi. I began to realize that I, too, had enjoyed myself immensely and I decided what perfect theater companions Luigi and Rina are. She, especially, was extremely amusing all the way to her house, where we accompanied her. She made elaborate fun of everything: the audience, the play, the starring actress—whom she could parody beautifully, pushing up the sleeves of her dress, running her hand with exaggerated nervousness through her hair.

I thought, too, how amazingly smart Rina looked last night. I really don't see how she manages it, since Luigi assures me she is telling the truth when she talks about not having a penny. Yet she always dresses with that impressive simplicity that is usually the mark of real style and high cost. But I think you feel about Rina instinctively that, in spite of anything, she would continue to get along, without being really seriously affected. If it is true that she's mad, then it must be also true that there is a special Providence for the mad.

An interesting thing that Luigi said afterward: we were discussing the silliness of the play's plot and I said that I thought that the boy had a rather violent reaction to his discovery of being illegitimate—going off to Africa and so on.

"Ridiculous," Luigi said at once. "Why, the intelligent thing to do in a situation like that is what Ugo Marinucci did. He was absolutely delighted, promptly moved out of the house and in with his real father, changed his name, and felt fine. His supposed father died shortly after that, his mother and real father married and everything was settled."

"Except," Rina added, "that his mother went crazy and talks about nothing but the lives of the saints."

"That doesn't mean anything. Ugo still did the right thing," Luigi insisted.

"Oh, absolutely," Rina agreed.

I realized a bit later that we had been discussing all this—what to do if you discover you're a bastard—in the most normal way, as if we were deciding the best thing to do for a toothache or how to make a long-distance phone call.

Another thing I noticed last night: Rina has finally given up trying to speak English to me. I feel much more at home with her, as if I weren't really a foreigner at all.

Friday.

Luigi has something that I haven't and probably never shall have: real maturity. He seems completely beyond the sort of fits of childishness or pique that attack me regularly. Nothing disturbs or stirs him to the point where he might become ridiculous.

I, on the other hand, have moments of folly that astonish me. This morning, for example, I went out to cash a check; and as I was walking along the street, watching the people and the cars as they passed, I was seized by a sudden, unreasonable happiness. And I wanted to proclaim myself to the people that passed me without noticing me; I wanted to make myself known, stopping some passing gentleman, some calm old lady, and shout: "I have seen the Pyramids at night"—something perfectly mad like that, or "I nearly died once in the Red Sea," or "I am twenty-four years old and have been in a war." And then, as my interlocutor would turn to go, I would cry after him, "And I will do these things again, and many more."

Of course, I wouldn't really shout these things. I walked on—outwardly sane—to the American

Express, cashed my check, stopped at a bookshop and bought a magazine, then went my way.

But this self-restraint isn't maturity, any more than is the occasional feeling that I am no longer young. Age and maturity are not the same. I will continue always to walk along the street, maintaining sometimes forcibly a normal exterior; but Luigi is different: the street means nothing to him; he is at home in all streets.

Later.

As I reread some of these notes, I feel that I am being terribly unjust to Luigi; he does not appear in his true self. I dwell on his laziness and his inertia, but I never mention his incredible personal charm, the gift he has for making me laugh, or for making me think. The gift is the more surprising because he apparently is unaware of it; he throws it away with his typical generosity.

Wednesday.

This morning an unplanned bit of sightseeing. I went for a stroll about ten o'clock through the gardens of the Villa Nazionale, enjoying in a peculiar way their quiet melancholy: the dusty, ill-kept walks, the disfigured statues. Then I suddenly noticed Rina walking toward me, swinging a string-bag of vegetables over her arm, her head high, unaware of her surroundings, and of me.

She seemed so completely out of place in that sad park that I all but laughed out loud. And it was good to see her; it made the morning an event in itself. I greeted her when she came up to me, then smiled at her surprise.

"Where are you going so intently?" I asked her.

"Home." She held up the bag. "And you?"

"No place." I waved my hand, indicating the gardens.

Then she suggested that, since we were so near there, we should go to the aquarium, and I agreed with enthusiasm. Rina's air of improvising seemed to glamorize things, and a trip to the aquarium became an adventure.

Certainly the rooms we went into then are like none other that I have ever seen: long, low, dark, and terribly humid. The floors are slippery and discolored. I felt as if we had gone in some contraption under the sea. Strange creatures of unrecognizable shapes glared out at us from their glass tanks. Everywhere we heard the sounds of bubbling and dripping.

I felt ill at ease, but Rina was delighted by everything. "Oh look, Bill," she would say, pointing to some particularly ugly creature. "Do you suppose he's unhappy?"

She drifted from tank to tank, pointing and commenting, and I thought how quickly she would make herself at home if we *were* beneath the sea. And I realized what a wonderful quality this adaptability is. I need much more of it myself.

When she saw I had stopped, in her impatience she grabbed my hand and pulled me away from the lampreys toward the sea-anemones. We stood together there, watching the pale, delicate organisms, half-plant, half-animal, waving and curling their long pastel-colored tendrils that look like mermaid's hair. And suddenly their strangeness made me more aware of my own, the foreigner's. I held Rina's hand a little tighter, as if I wanted to make myself felt *here,* a citizen.

And for a moment, I think, I felt impelled toward Rina, wanting her. Just for a moment, then one of us—it might have been I—moved on and we began talking again. Perhaps Rina didn't even notice it; at least she showed nothing.

But now, thinking the whole thing over (it happened only a few hours ago), I think I see clearly what was happening to me. *Then* the only thing that occurred to me was my own incapacity; after all, Rina is not simply an American college girl, and never,

126

never has been. Therefore, there would have been all sorts of practical considerations, usual things that I would not have known how to say or do. These little things assume a magnified importance.

More than that, though, I know now that it wasn't Rina herself I wanted; it was Naples. I wanted to be accepted here in some tangible, unforgettable way. Luigi the other day said of Sicily: "A place that is wonderful to visit, but only if you are in love." I think that is true perhaps of all Italy; and I *am* in love, but with no one individual. I am in love with this whole damn place.

Partly, too, Luigi's talks about his girl have influenced me without doubt. In some secret way I probably wanted to emulate him, to have some excitement of my own. How ridiculous this is, and yet how real. I could never tell any of this to N. I can imagine the reaction: the two of us discussing it all sanely, intelligently, probing my feelings, my emotional situation. Oddly enough, I feel I could tell the whole of it to Rina and she wouldn't raise an eyebrow. Of course, I never shall.

Friday.

Someday someone (perhaps I myself) will have to write a book on The Science of Traveling, or

127

perhaps The Art of Traveling. For traveling is more an art than a science, I suppose. It is a discipline, but not so exact as biology or chemistry. There are rules and fundamentals (expect nothing, accept everything), as there are in an art. One must master these, and then one must seek his own path.

Travel books always deal too strictly with places, views, details. But the important aspect of a voyage is what happens within the voyager. In real travel, the country one explores is himself. Speaking a foreign language, one examines what one says. In an unfamiliar tongue there are no commonplaces.

Note: idea for a book. A travel-novel in which the conflict, instead of being between the hero and the villain, is between the hero and the place.

Saturday.

I find myself becoming not only tolerant, but unconcerned about the various secret lives of people around here that Luigi narrates to me. Suddenly it seems to me perfectly natural that a wife should have a lover and a husband a mistress, that children should be illegitimate, that sweet old ladies should have lurid pasts. Every now and then, I realize with a certain shock this attitude of mine—but the astonishment is always with myself, never with the people that Luigi discusses.

Later.

Is this a good sign or not? I can't say. But it seems to me only a symptom of some larger change in my state of mind, some wider acceptance. It may be a kind of maturity, after all.

Sunday.

Sometimes these days when I am mentally criticizing Luigi, finding him lacking in moral determination, and calling him a drifter and an irresponsible— then another inner voice tells me to shut up. After all, it says to me, how are you any better? What are you doing here, if not drifting?

And for a moment I feel apologetic toward Luigi, as if I had no right to judge him. Of course, I don't; but at the same time, it is unnecessary for me to feel any guilt about it. Because Luigi is beyond all necessity of moral justification; he has no idea that he is neglecting some obligation or failing any mission.

As for my own justification, my own answers to the questions that Luigi would never ask me—what can I say to defend myself? That I held down a job for a year, got a college degree, wrote a bad novel that nobody would publish? These do not seem to suffice, or at least they don't satisfy *me*. But, at the same time,

129

I feel that there is a defense for me. Even the very feeling that I should have a justification is perhaps the beginning of one. Ah, if I could only feel as Luigi does. But that is one of the ineradicable differences between us that may sometimes make it a little difficult for us to get along together.

Monday.

Rosaria, the maid, was fired this morning. I was disturbed when I learned about it, but Luigi assured me that she would be re-hired by dinnertime, and it turned out he was right. When I came back from the post office around one, she was setting the table as if nothing had happened.

Signora Fabbri is, in everything, excitable, so hardly a morning passes without some kind of fracas between her and Rosaria or her and Maria, the cook. They wrangle over everything and anything, usually when Luigi and I are just waking up, so that the day always starts off with excitement. It's a little like waking up and finding yourself in the ring, half-way through the first round of a boxing match.

This morning's fight was considerably more agitated than anything I had seen before. It was concerned with 500 lire change from something that Rosaria, who is scrupulously honest, had been sent out to buy. She came back without change and the signora insisted that she had forgotten it; Rosaria said she had been given a 500 lire note; the signora said, no, a 1000 lire note. From then on it was anybody's verdict.

The signora repeated that she wasn't accusing Rosaria of stealing, only of forgetting her change. But poor Rosaria wasn't to be mollified: her shrill, piercing screams of rage must have been audible all the way to Tripoli. And Signora Fabbri didn't take things quietly, either. They moved back and forth through our room and the salon, using Luigi and me as an audience. Luigi, who was completely indifferent and refused to share my interest in it all.

Repeating and repeating the same sentences ("1000, I tell you," "You want to make a fool of me," "Yes," "No,"), the two of them grew more and more heated, until at last the Signora—as much to change refrain as anything else, I suppose—"I won't have you screaming in my house this way." And Rosaria shouted, "I'll go, then."

And so she went. But not until she had come into our room, let out one last incoherent scream of fury, thrown down her dishtowel as if it were a test-tube filled with high explosive, and stamped out, her wooden soles clacking through the rooms and along the outer hall.

131

The signora, quite done in by the whole fray, sank down on the foot of Luigi's bed and looked to us for affirmation. "Completely crazy," she said..." servants... I do more work than they do..."

"My mother has nothing to do but argue," Luigi said to me in English, "she doesn't read or write letters, since all her friends are here, so she argues. With me, or with the servants, or with my father. It's her way of exercise, like swimming is for me..."

I nodded, and the signora seemed to think that we were approving so she got up very happily, went out and buttered us each a piece of bread.

Rosaria, too, seemed content, when I found her at dinnertime. She was singing, in that sharp, unbelievable voice of hers, and setting the table with little flourishes as if the Pope were expected as a guest. She had that pleased, exhilarated air that Luigi has when he runs up the steps from the beach.

Tuesday.

I am in bed, laid up. And the reason for it is so stupid that I am furious. Last night we went to call on some friends of Luigi's and, afterwards as I stepped down from the bus in front of the Palazzo, I put my foot into an uneven place in the street and fell, twisting my ankle.

It must have been ridiculous to see. Anyway Luigi laughed heartily, and I became enraged, since I was sitting there in the street, my eyes filled with spontaneous tears from the sudden pain. Finally—after a moment only—Luigi realized that I had hurt myself and became all solicitude, helped me down the stairs, put me to bed, and applied a cold compress to my ankle. Later, when the Fabbris came in, he told them what had happened, and the signora insisted that the doctor should be called this morning.

He has just left. A comic-opera doctor with white beard and pince-nez, who clucked to himself, and poked at my foot, as if he were performing part of a kabbalistic rite. In the end he said I must stay in bed, absolutely not move, and continue applications of *acqua vegeto-minerale.* The name of this fascinates me and I can hardly wait until Luigi comes back from town with it; I picture it as a kind of vegetable soup, but fizzing like mineral water.

But I am in a really black mood. The doctor, for all his ridiculousness, brought out all my nationalism and I wished heartily for a "good, American doctor," equipped with all the latest gadgets and drugs, who would talk to me reassuringly, tell me the names of all my foot-bones, and suggest an X-ray just to be sure. And, beyond my dissatisfaction with the doctor, I am

133

still angry with Luigi, who is taking the whole thing much too lightly. The fact that I have to stay in bed for a week seems nothing to him; to me it seems a real disaster. Suddenly all the things that I have wanted to do in Naples loom up in front of me, and I am filled with regret for not having done any of them.

What will I *do* in these days? I have read all the English books I brought with me and all that Luigi has, and I am too out of patience to bother with Italian books, that take more time and concentration. Luigi, in his thoughtlessness, doesn't seem to feel that he has to stay home and entertain me; this morning he went out as soon as the doctor came and will not be back until lunch time (he might have hurried a bit, if only to bring back my *acqua v-m*, so that I could begin the applications). Already I am going mad with boredom and self-pity.

Later.

The *acqua vegeto-minerale* was rather a disappointment. Not a bit as I imagined. A dull, thick white liquid like some kind of hand lotion. Luigi had the sense to buy some absorbent cotton and a bandage so that I can put the stuff on conveniently and wrap it into place. There is an ungodly lump behind my ankle and the entire foot is swollen and discolored. I make experimental movements with it, which are no doubt a bad thing, but I can't resist. I have to do something, even if only wiggle my foot.

Wednesday.

My foot looks worse this morning. I unwrapped the bandage and took off the absorbent cotton to have a good look, and I must say it's an unusually repulsive sight. The toes are a pale blue color; the top of the foot a hideous purple which blends to a kind of amber-orange around the ankle. I glared at it, fascinated, for a while, then hastily applied some more of that white stuff and rewrapped the whole thing.

Now I am lying back in my bed, as I have been all day, letting my mind wander. I have reached out and thrown open the window, and the sea breeze is ruffling across my bed, as if I were sitting in a deck-chair aboard ship. Everything seems in motion, in contrast to my idleness. I hear the fishermen, talking in their boats as they row past; then the voices grow thinner, then fade out like smoke.

Rosaria is in the kitchen, clearing up and preparing supper. She has the radio turned on, but I can barely hear an occasional strain of music; sometimes a voice laughs for a moment, then is stopped. This makes me feel lonely; I would prefer to hear nothing.

135

I don't see how I am going to stand this for a week. Yesterday evening, to while away time, I wrote letters to everyone I could think of; but it will be weeks before any answers come. In the meantime I can, I suppose, continue to write in this diary. But what will I write, if nothing happens to me? Damn my foot, anyway.

Thursday.

This morning I decided that I should leave. As soon as my foot clears up and I can get my things together. I should be gone by the end of next week, Friday—or a Saturday, at the latest. Suddenly to set a fixed day for my departure has had a good effect on me; some of my irritability has gone now. Why has it taken me so long to come to this? What has kept me here? I think I have been waiting until I felt free of this place, until there was some calm in me that resisted, or resolved the city's disturbance of my spirit.

Because that is what it has been: I have been trying to solve the problem of living in Naples, among people that I loved, who upset me, who seemed to be attacking me by their very passiveness, their nonchalance (the Italian *noncuranza* is a better word).

And the answer is, finally, so simple. A phrase of Nietzsche comes to me again and again these days; he says that we should leave life "blessing it, but not in love with it." This is the way I should leave Naples. I have felt all along, unconsciously, that I had to decide about these people, this way of life. And now I have realized that there is no need for me to judge it, to say if it is right or wrong. I know that it is not *my* way, but I can bless it, accept it as it is, study it, and—now that I know this—leave it, wiser, I hope, and freer.

When Luigi came in for dinner, after I had thought this out, I didn't try to tell him this. I only said that I thought I should be leaving soon, that I would miss Naples, that I would want to come back someday, that I felt my stay here had done me good. He agreed with all this, and said he was sorry to see me go. I think he understands all that I didn't say.

Later.

Decision has a salutary effect on me. I seem to have no problems at all; nothing bothers me. If I am left alone (as I am now), I amuse myself by day-dreaming about Rome, imagining the trip up, the city (which I never saw during the war), my arrival. I picture myself arriving in front of St. Peter's or the Coliseum—how can one imagine a bus station in Rome? It would be like picturing the customs house in Paradise.

137

And yet it isn't the actual trip up that excites me so much. As a matter of fact I don't like to dwell on the business of packing, getting tickets, cabs, reservations. I prefer to envision myself already there, settled, meeting new people, seeing different streets.

Saturday.

This morning, to pass the time and as a kind of mental exercise, I assigned myself the task of writing a description of the apartment. It didn't come out quite as I had expected—like all my writing that I intend to be spontaneous, it is quite literary and a little stilted. But I shall copy it into this diary just as a record:

As I lie in bed now, the sea is at my back, beyond the closed window. But I can hear it, and almost feel it, when it strikes regularly against the wall of the building below. Its noise and motion are in sharp contrast with the room that faces me, quiet and deserted and sparsely furnished. I look at the bed across from me, neatly made, and the table, and the desk. All are dark: the heavy counterpane, the solid, ancient furniture. Even the walls are covered with a brown stuff that gives the room a perpetual air of twilight.

Some of Luigi's books, which cover half the far wall, are bound in bright colors, and they—appropriately—give the place light, as at this moment do the

138

white sheets of his unfinished novel scattered across the top of the chest of drawers.

The rooms beyond are silent as well at this mid-morning hour. The family is out visiting and the servants have gone on errands, the daily round of shopping and bargaining, which they recount at length to the signora in the hour of preparing dinner. But now the large main room, which is both dining room and salon, is empty. The shutters are closed so the mahogany table does not gleam, in spite of its polish. The heavy, uncomfortable chairs are lost in darkness, like the formal sofas. The paintings, I imagine, are squares of black now: those eighteenth-century Nea-politan still-lifes, so crammed with details: vine-leaves, and bitten apples, and melons bursting with seeds.

And the signora's bedroom. I think of it as hers, though she shares it with her husband, because of the brocaded walls covered with religious pictures, cruci-fixes—which Signor Fabbri, who shares Luigi's scepticism about religion, would not have put there. He would approve, however, of the ranks of family photographs that cover all the surfaces, the dressing table and bureau and escritoire; he, like his wife, has a strong sense of family.

Only the kitchen is filled with sunlight now. They do not bother to close the shutters there since there is nothing to fade or to spoil. Rosaria and Maria have cleaned and put away everything. The marble surfaces all shine in the light; the only odor is of the sea, which blows in from the back terrace, where the ice-box is kept and the strings of onions and garlic and the baskets of vegetables. The washing-woman has hung the damp clothes there, and the ironing-woman will come tomorrow to press them.

As I think of these rooms now it occurs to me how unlike they are the people who inhabit them. A stranger coming to this apartment at this hour of the morning could not picture the signora, explosive and affectionate, or the quiet husband, or the complex literary-sensual son, or the younger black sheep, off at Capri, who has lived his whole youth here without leaving a trace. That is the irony of houses: they inhabit us more than we inhabit them. And when I leave after six weeks or so, this room will be in me forever, and I have not left a scratch on a wall for a souvenir.

Thursday.

Partly, I suppose, in celebration of my recovery, and partly because I will be leaving Naples soon, I have spent a great portion of the last few days walking around the city—not so much looking in windows or staring into the faces of the people who pass me (as I did when I was first here) but more absorbed in myself, as if trying to judge, to define the effect that merely *being* in this city has upon me.

It is indefinable, and yet it exists. I do not feel this way in another place—this conflicting sensation of half-belonging and half-withdrawing. Now that I have made up my mind to continue my journey, it is as if part of me had already left.

There is always this paradox in traveling. One moves twice; a journey is a double experience: the outer, physical removal from one place to another, but beyond that, or within it, the inner journey that one makes in one's spirit.

The two journeys are disproportionate. The tripper can travel for miles from Topeka to Tashkent, and not move an inch in his soul. Or the real traveler can walk across the street and have a lifetime's worth of experience. These are not accidental matters, nor unrelated: certainly "travel broadens"—or rather, it deepens. The exterior voyage stimulates the interior one. But the voyager must attend to both, to miss neither.

I am fond of the voyage metaphor that is so popular—"life is a voyage"—but I think we should consider carefully its converse. A voyage is life. the microcosm. One is born at departure, matures, grows, learns, experiences in the trip, and when he arrives safely home again, the voyage is dead, but if he has followed it well, it is immortalized in its own eternity.

And so, like some Oriental, at the moment I am dying, my journey around Naples is coming to an end. But, at the same time, I am about to be born again—every label on a suitcase, every ticket-stub is a reminder. I am both reluctant and impatient.

Last entry.

I am writing this in Formia. The bus has stopped here for an hour to allow everyone to eat lunch. Having eaten the rolls and cheese that the signora gave me this morning, I am filling the time by recording this, my last picture of Naples. It is a good idea, I believe, to write it down before I get to Rome and am struck again by newness and unfamiliarity (I am already feeling the traveler's excitement: I wonder about the man who shares my seat and the old lady across from me, who is right now eating a long staff of bread and some foul-smelling salami).

My departure was confused as my arrival had been. Luigi insisted on getting up to see me off, then took so long deciding which shoes to wear that I was sure I was going to miss the bus altogether. We had a hard time finding a taxi; I couldn't remember the name of the street where the bus company's office is, and I nearly went crazy until I thought of looking on the ticket.

Naturally Luigi remained calm through all this, and—it turned out—with complete reason, since the bus left three-quarters of an hour late. It was raining when we got there, just a thin drizzle, but it is the beginning of winter, I know. From now on the rain will be more frequent there and heavier, too. I left the right day.

Luigi helped me put my bags on the rack, then stood outside under the window—oblivious of the rain—and talked to me, assuring me that he would be coming to Rome soon, himself, as soon as a few more things were arranged. I didn't bother to show enthusiasm, even though I would like him to come; I will miss him in Rome. But I know he won't come there. Then, when we left, and I saw him walking through the rain back towards the Palazzo and the sea, I couldn't say that he is wrong.

The very simplicity and nakedness of man's life in the primitive ages imply this advantage at least, that they left him still but a sojourner in nature. When he was refreshed with food and sleep he contemplated his journey again. He dwelt, as it were, in a tent in this world...

THOREAU, *Walden*, page 31

143

A*n Afterword.*

The events recorded in the preceding pages are, for the most part, true. They actually took place, more or less in the year and month ascribed to them. A young American named Bill really did live with a Neapolitan family, consisting of two parents, two sons, a unique maid of all work, and numerous collateral relations and relationships. That family lived in a few spacious rooms in the historic, crumbling Palazzo Donn'Anna on the cape of Posillipo, with the classic postcard view of Vesuvius and Capri, and the Sorrento coastline in the distance.

But the specific dates assigned to these diary entries are a fiction. In fact, the diary itself is a fiction. You must not imagine young Bill curled up in his bed during the long Neapolitan siesta hours or awake at night dutifully recording his Naples days in an inseparable notebook before turning out the light and falling asleep, to the singing of the fishermen drifting over the bay.

Nothing of the sort. After his confused Neapoli-

tan days—with their encounters, their frustrations,
their surprises and shocks—Bill was much too exhausted to pick up a pen; and during the post-prandial
hours, unused as he was to regular wine-drinking (a
habit he lost no time in acquiring), his thoughts were
far too muddled to permit or deserve recording. In
any case, during those weeks Bill was concerned
exclusively with life and with himself; he could de-
vote scant thought to literature. In the midst of
Naples, overwhelmed by its loud, sweet, aromatic
immediacy, he was unable to see himself or his surroundings in any perspective. Detachment was the
least of his concerns. His life was totally centripetal.

Some weeks later, however, he moved to Rome,
preparing to embark at last on what he thought
would be his real Italian life; and then, in some
curious reaction to his new and quite different con-
text, he began to re-examine his Neapolitan days, a
life that—recent though it was—appeared now more
and more unreal, dream-like, and rich as it inevitably
receded into the past.

In Rome, on his own much of the time, Bill had
things to do, a plan to execute, resolutions to follow:
first of all, he had determined, he would perfect his
Italian, he would meet famous writers (on Capri he
had already made friends with Alberto Moravia, a

good start), he would have a dazzling love affair, and —supreme goal—he would write a novel. Or rather, as he privately thought of it; he would write *his* novel, as if the story were already there, staked out for him somewhere in the ether, waiting for him to capture it and fix it on paper.

Except for the love-affair, most of these goals were somehow achieved, but, of course, not in the form they had assumed in the dream.

Thanks to some Neapolitan friends, Bill found a bed in a cheap, gloomy pensione; there were two beds in the room, the other occupied by Achille, a working actor, who regularly received his lovely, patient girlfriend there in the afternoons, while Bill was obliged to take long walks or, funds permitting, sit and read in a caffé. Mornings, Achille slept late, so in effect Bill was able to use his half of the room only for sleep.

Fortunately, his friends who shared the big room across the hall, the former salon, went out early and stayed out: Peppino, to his job at the Italian Radio, and Mario, to his classes at the Accademia di Arte Drammatica. So, once Bill had come back from his morning espresso at the corner of the piazza, he could move into the great dark room, open his typewriter, and set about working on the—his—novel.

147

Today, after fifty years, I can hardly be expected to remember the plot: it involved a murder, an unnamed island (based on Capri, where I had been the previous month), an unhappy marriage, some colorful tourists, and a certain amount of soul-searching—I forget whose soul—and sensitive scene-painting. It bored me even then, as it was later to bore the dozen editors to whom it was fruitlessly submitted.

Often, I would foresake the desk for one of the cots, where I could stretch out and look at a book or doze. Still unable to read Italian with much satisfaction, I probably stuck with my then favorites, English novelists like Henry Green and Graham Greene, Rex Warner, and—my idol—Christopher Isherwood. I had discovered Isherwood a few years before, during the war, when in the bookshops of the Middle East, English-language books were surprisingly accessible, so I was able to devour not only the Berlin books, but also *Lions and Shadows*. While narrating some of his career disappointments, Isherwood made writing seem such total, unalloyed fun that I made up my mind—I remember the specific moment of the decision, among the temples of Baalbek—that I would be a writer, though, truth to tell, I myself didn't find the act of writing much fun at all.

Surely inspired by *Goodbye to Berlin*, and perhaps

148

also by my life-companion book Thoreau's *Walden*,
at some point in that Roman November I began to
invent a Naples diary. I meant to put down on paper
not only my encounter with the city that fascinated
me—and still does fascinate me—but also my self-
investigation, inspired by that period of total freedom,
not only from school, family, but also from any real
responsibility. In Rome now, at a safe distance from
the siren shore of Posillipo, I could achieve, at least
partially, a detachment from recent events but also
from myself. In those weeks, I realized, I was grow-
ing; and, amazingly, I could almost observe the process.
Like Alice, I had drunk the magic potion labeled
"drink me," and I was shooting up, head and shoulders above my former self.

So while the novel had labored forward, sentence after plodding sentence, *A Tent in This World*—
title from Thoreau, of course—came flowing forth,
as if spontaneously. I wrote without any scheme, no
outline, no parallel notebook (my novel, of course,
had inspired a Gide-like *cahier*, in which I discussed
my cardboard characters with myself at numbing
length). As I wrote about one Neapolitan episode,
assigning it a fictitious date, another would rush to my
mind, complete with dialogue.

Within a couple of months, I had finished. I did

a minimum of revising, added a few scenes that occurred to me belatedly; and there it was, a manuscript of around a hundred pages, an impossible length: too short for a book, too long for a magazine. With a sigh, I put it in my suitcase with my summer clothes, and I returned to the eternal novel.

But at some point in that late winter, an Italian friend, the painter Dario Cecchi, took me to meet Marguerite Caetani—neé Chapin—a New England-born, Roman princess, who in the Palazzo Caetani, located in the mediaeval Via delle Botteghe Oscure, published an elegant international review, which took its name from the street. The fact that in the same street the national Communist Party headquarters was located was something the Principessa aristocratically ignored. So while, for most Italians, "Botteghe Oscure" simply meant Communists; for the enlightened few, it meant a rich semi-annual publication, in several languages, where the world-famous (Spender, Auden, Char, Dylan Thomas) mingled with the unknown or soon-to-be-known (Muriel Spark, Pier Paolo Pasolini).

But more important than the review was the society that collected around it. Marguerite would have scorned a pompous word like "salon," but how else can you define that spacious, warmly welcoming

150

living room, where over a cup of tea, you could meet any of the above writers, along with painters (Marguerite had been painted by Bonnard and Vuillard; her daughter by Sickert), musicians (Prince Roffredo, then close to ninety, was a composer, his god-father was Liszt), distinguished anti-Fascists, and—when Marguerite allowed him to invite them—a scattering of the Prince's aristocratic relatives?

Officially, the editor of the review was Giorgio Bassani—future author of *The Garden of the Finzi-Continis*—but, at this time, perhaps better known as a poet and writer of an occasional novella. Giorgio— we soon became first-name friends—was instrumental in bringing many new writers into the Caetani orbit, but the Principessa herself, in her own apparently random way, actually kept a close and critical eye on the magazine's content.

She proceeded largely by instinct, following her likes and dislikes. One would not have thought Theodore Roethke her kind of poet, but she liked the great, burly man who overflowed the little slipper-chair by her fireplace, and she published him generously. And, I have to say, she also liked me. One of the constant problems of *Botteghe Oscure* was proof-reading—especially the English and French texts—as the hard-working Italian printers did their best, but still they tended to break words oddly (even "th-e" on occasion) and to make two new errors for every old one they corrected. At least for the English section, I was able to help her and so I spent many afternoons and evenings at the shop of the genial and intellectual printer De Luca. Errors continued to recur, but on a somewhat less devastating scale.

One day, when she asked me what I was writing, I told her about my Naples diary; she asked to see it. After reading it, to my bewildered delight, she said she wanted to run it in the magazine. I felt bound to point out the excessive length—nothing that long had ever appeared in *Botteghe Oscure*—but she dismissed the problem with a wave of the hand. "We'll print it in smaller type."

And so, *A Tent in This World* appeared in number V of *Botteghe Oscure,* dated simply Roma MCML. I was in distinguished company; the Italian contributors to that issue included Carlo Levi, Mario Soldati, Bassani himself, Rocco Scotellaro; the French were represented by Valéry (an old friend of Marguerite's), her great favorite René Char, Bernard Courtin, Philippe Jaccottet, and others; while in the large English-language section there were David Gascoyne, Edwin Muir, Kathleen Raine, Vernon Watkins, James Agee, Isabel Bolton (pen-name of Marguerite's cousin

Mary Miller), Richard Eberhart, Louis Zukofsky, Richard Wilbur, and—last of all—William Fense Weaver.

Yes, so far I have referred to this author chiefly in the third person as "he" or as "Bill." But professionally—insofar as he was a professional—he chose to go by the pretentious triple name. And so it is all the easier for me to see him now as a separate, slightly alien person. Who was this William Fense Weaver? Well, if you have read the preceding pages, you will have learned a lot about him from his Neapolitan diary. He was a personable, well-educated youth, who had long since lost his Southern accent, but never his Southern sociability. He had an insatiable curiosity, a willingness to suffer discomfort or even boredom to satisfy it. And he himself had no idea who he was or where he was going.

He had published a couple of stories in American national magazines, a poem in the then prestigious *Poetry*, Chicago, and he was beginning to do a little translating, largely to make some money, for he had no income beyond scant savings from a year's teaching and the small sums he could scrape together (then miraculously increased by the largesse of the Principessa).

The diary reinforced his ambition and also won

him some Italian admirers. But it didn't make his novel any better. He actually finished it, sent it to an agent, and—supreme folly—began another. He finished that one, too; and it also went the rounds of American publishers. The trouble was that these novels were not impossibly dreadful; they were decently written, with the occasional page of attractive dialogue, the occasional bold, effective metaphor. Honestly, they were almost good; but they were not in any way necessary. There was no need for anyone to read them or, for that matter, to write them.

As they circulated in vain, his work as a translator slowly developed into a serious profession and he began to take it more seriously, discovering the challenges of the craft and the satisfaction to be derived from facing them. Eventually it became clear that three names were too many (how could an "Elsa Morante" be translated by a "William Fense Weaver"?). So he dropped the middle name and became me. And —with a huge sigh of relief—he dropped the whole idea of writing novels.

When *A Tent in This World* came out, he assumed it would appear only in English and he felt safe from any Neapolitan recrimination: but the Principessa had a firm policy of printing, in a separate opuscule, translations of the magazine's contents; thus, in a makeshift Italian version, *Una tenda nel mondo* was distributed along with its original. It was hardly a secret that the "Luigi" of the diary was, in reality, the brilliant young Italian novelist Raffaele LaCapria, my first Italian friend, a man of infinite humor, compassion, and aplomb, who took my not-always-flattering depiction of himself as the affectionate and amusing portrait it was meant to be. His younger brother ("Cesare" in the preceding pages), though he knew no English, somehow managed to learn the contents of my *Tent* and found them hilarious.

Cesare—or "Pelos," to give him his eternal childhood nickname—was and is a great tease. So, on the Easter after the publication of the diary, when I went down to Naples for the ritual big family dinner, he waited until the dessert arrived, a deliriously successful *pastiera* with a dozen blended savors, and turned to his ancient grandmother, shouting to make himself heard:

"Nonna! Bill here has written a book. All about us! He says you could have been the mistress of the Pope!"

For a moment I wondered if there were some way I could commit suicide by sheer will-power. But the Nonna, seated at my side, leaned towards me, grasped my forearm, and said defiantly: "It's true!"

155

WILLIAM WEAVER

And, without hesitation, she told me the story again; her youthful innocence and beauty, the grand party in Rome, the *papabile* cardinal, the unequivocal "certain look." Her now-regretted self-denial.

Then it dawned on me that, while I thought my diary was the story of a straightforward, ordinary American youth confronted by an eccentric Neapolitan family, the LaCaprias thought it rather the story of a normal Neapolitan family who welcome an eccentric and rather simple-minded American youth, who misunderstands everything. Not long ago, Raffaele —now one of Italy's most admired and thoughtful writers—wrote a light, reminiscent piece about Naples and about *Una Tenda nel mondo,* attributing to me all sorts of Jamesian complexities. It is a charming piece, but now he is the one who hasn't understood: I was not nearly as simple-minded as I made myself out in the diary, I wanted to establish a contrast between the complex Neapolitans and the anonymous diarist. I was trying to be Isherwood. Actually, if there is a fictional character in the diary, it is "Bill."

For several decades William Fense Weaver lay low. Then, a few years ago, a generous colleague at Bard College, the poet Robert Kelly, organized a series of readings by writers teaching or living near the College. He kindly asked me to be one of their

156

number, and since I assumed he did not want to hear me read a travel piece on Ancona from the *Times* or a discussion of *Un ballo in maschera* from the San Francisco Opera program—the sort of writing I mostly do nowadays—I thought to revive my long-silent alter ego, and I read some excerpts from the never-quite-forgotten (I admit) Neapolitan diary. The reading went well, Robert's totally convincing enthusiasm inspired me first to show the text to an Italian publisher, who commissioned a new translation and brought it out in an attractive edition, then to Robert's own publisher Bruce McPherson, a convinced and effective advocate of Italian letters. Hence the present reissue, when—whatever its literary virtues—the text now has the value of a historical document.

The document is authentic. I may have felt an occasional twinge of temptation, an instinct to reach for the revising pencil, but I have resisted. Nothing here, apart from a few corrected typos, has been changed. This is completely the work of William Fense. I would make only one addition. To the dedication, beside the name of my friend of half a century, Raffaele LaCapria, I would have you see also the name of Ilaria Occhini, who has shared his life and, with it, our friendship.

—*William Weaver*

A Tent in This World

is published in a first edition
of 1500 numbered copies
and 26 lettered copies
signed by the author.

Copy 652